The Civil War

at Home

Dustin McKissen

**Working Class
Books**

Working Class Books

Published by: Working Class Books
Cover Design by: Melanie Layer-Gaskell

Lyrics to "Common Ground" used with permission of Frank Turner. Copyright 2018 by Frank Turner.

ISBN: 978-1-7327693-2-8 (Paperback)
ISBN: 978-1-7327693-3-5 (Ebook)

Distributed by: Working Class Books
                    1001 State Street #907
                    Erie, Pennsylvania 16501

For my wife Megan,
who is the strongest person I've ever met.

All characters in this book are fictional.

With the exception of Donald Trump.

If it were just the best of us
Against the rest of us
It wouldn't even be an argument at all
It would be a victory or
A Spanish Civil War
But I'm really not so sure that is the way it is at all

If we are to find a way to live
Then we need to build ourselves a bridge
And if we were to build ourselves that bridge
We could meet in the middle and forgive

If all we are is dust to dust
Then in the end what's left of us
Are the traces of the way we treat the ones we meet
And the ones who trouble us
Are the greatest test of us

Frank Turner
"Common Ground"

Part I: The Breaking Point

Chapter One

Marina

Even with everything happening, with her blood everywhere and me hoping the kids wouldn't see and not remembering if they had already gotten on the school bus and Kevin screaming and running toward Rick's house with something in his hand and Rick running from his garage toward Kevin, I had one clear thought:

I didn't even know we owned a gun.

Kate

Most of the blood was off me by the time I woke up. I had scrubbed and scrubbed in the truck stop shower the night before, getting it off my arms and hands, but there was still a little blood on my pajama bottoms.

You would think the cashier would call the police. A woman shows up with blood all over her and tears in her eyes, asking for a shower in the middle of the night. It seems like a pretty good time to put your phone down and pay attention to what's happening. It might even be a good time to use your phone to make an actual phone call. The cashier didn't call anyone, though. Maybe all the blood and tears scared him. Or maybe if you're working the graveyard shift for eight bucks an hour your give-a-hoot is fairly low.

Maybe in this day and age, a bloody stranger is no longer cause for alarm. Or, maybe God works in mysterious ways.

You never really know what that saying means until you're a grown woman getting back into dirty pajamas after showering off blood at a truck stop. Putting dirty underwear back on after a hot shower is the worst. But it's not like I carry clean underwear in my car. It's not like this is how I thought our story would end. It's not like I prepared accordingly. No one plans on spending the night in the bloody front seat of an old Dodge Neon we haven't even paid off.

If I had planned this, there would have at least been a pair of fresh underwear in the glovebox, rather than a bloody butcher knife. But no one plans for something like this.

Part II:
The Build-Up

Chapter Two

Kevin

Except for the annual neighborhood party Rick and Kate hosted every fall, my interaction with my neighbor mostly consisted of meeting in the street that separates our houses to talk about work. Rick would talk about the janitorial supplies business. Rick made his living selling toilet paper. I felt self-conscious talking about my white-collar consulting job around Rick, so I usually just mumbled a few generalities. We would end the conversation by making our usual half-hearted promise to get a beer together. It was a promise we never kept.

Rick probably thought the same thing I did, that the half-hearted commitment reflected our half-hearted feelings about each other. We were neighborly enough to be cordial, but not enough to spend any time getting to really know each other. Rick has four daughters. I have two daughters and a son.

We are both fathers. That is something we share. I would occasionally fake enough interest in baseball to carry on a conversation about Rick's favorite team. It wasn't a conversation I particularly enjoyed, but it was something we did. We were men. That's what men do, or at least what we're expected to do. Honestly though, I couldn't care less about baseball.

Most of the time we didn't talk at all. We just waved, the sort of neighborly wave where you raise one hand before you go back to doing whatever it was you were doing before.

"Howdy, Kevin," Rick would shout as he raised one arm from his lawnmower.

"Hello, Rick," I would say, resting my briefcase against my shoe so I could wave back.

When we talked at all, howdy and hello was the extent of it. That was our routine. There were limits to our friendship, in other words.

For a while, Rick and I also had a cordial enough Facebook relationship. Like our real-life relationship, being cordial on Facebook depended on each of us ignoring the other. Facebook served an important purpose for us. It was through Facebook that we realized there was no need to get that beer, because we already knew each other: Rick was a knuckle-dragging conservative Jesus-freak janitorial supply salesperson with what appeared to be a passionate man crush on Sean Hannity. I was a Godless liberal marketing consultant with too many new cars and a Mexican wife who wasn't really that

Mexican but was Mexican enough for Rick to hate and stereotype and never bother to get to know. Facebook confirmed we were what each of us had always assumed we were.

That was okay though, because we were just neighbors. It's not like we were brothers. I usually forgot Rick was even there, except for one day every October when Marina made her famous bloody peanut butter eyeballs and we crossed the street to eat mushy, boiled hotdogs in Rick's backyard the weekend before Halloween. Rick's party was really a Halloween party, but being a bit of a Christian fanatic, he had to call it a Fall Harvest party—as though Rick or any of his well-off Christian friends actually ever harvested anything.

Or, I mean we used to get together to awkwardly celebrate a nonexistent Fall Harvest by eating peanut butter eyeballs and gross hotdogs while pretending that—because Jesus wouldn't approve of it—we aren't actually celebrating Halloween.

But that was before Donald Trump. Before Rick became a Nazi.

When that happened, I decided we were done with Fall Harvest, for good.

Rick

I am not what Kevin thinks I am. I am not racist. I am not sexist. I am not a Nazi. I am not a displaced angry blue-collar factory worker who's tried to drown his sorrows in heroin. I am not uneducated. I went to college. Truth be told, I come from a family that believes you go to college right after you finish high school, whether you want to or not. It's just what we do in our family. Even if you end up selling toilet paper to looney bins, you do it with a college degree.

"If nothing else, son, a degree is a safety net," my father said. "It will catch you when you fall. Professionally speaking."

Ha! I didn't graduate with honors, but my GPA was something my parents were proud of. My parents also taught me success isn't measured by grades and degrees. Success should be measured by the things in life that really matter. I am proud of all four of my girls. I am proud of my wife. I am proud of my neighborhood. I am proud of my country. I am proud of the Lord and His place in my life.

Me and Kate have been so blessed. The only thing I struggle to be proud of is myself. In my early twenties, I was diagnosed with an illness I have to manage. It's a mental illness, but I'm not crazy. It's not like I hear voices or anything. Ours isn't an easy life, but we make it work. We have a big family that's spread all over town. We aren't likely to go hungry. Lord willing, we make it work. We make it work because though we live in the suburbs, it feels like a small town. It feels like the type of small town America is losing. It's a place where people come together when times get hard. People step up here. They get each other's back.

I certainly had Kevin's back.

Right after he and Marina moved here, his mom committed suicide. They had to go back to wherever it is he came from to take care of things. Kate and I took care of their kids while Kevin and Marina flew home to handle his mom's funeral. They are good kids, too. They cleaned up their mac n' cheese plates and did every chore we asked them to do. They answered questions by looking us directly in the eyes. I know Kevin and Marina do not have a relationship with their Lord and Savior, Jesus Christ. How a man without a relationship with the Lord can raise such well-behaved children is something I'll never understand.

But questions like that are above this janitorial supply salesman's pay grade.

One more thing about me: I am a Donald Trump supporter, but I didn't start out that way. I was once a Bush guy: Sr., Jr., and Jeb. Then, after my career hit some bumps, I got more informed. I wanted to know what was happening to people like me. I always kept up with politics for my job at the paper, but for the first time in my life I felt like I saw the light. Trump helped me realize how much our country has changed. And not for the better.

Things were okay around here for a long time, but now they're not. Trump fights back. That's what I love about him. Now I'm a MAGA guy. For the first time in my life I even have a bumper sticker on my car. Our MAGA sticker tells the world who we are and what matters most to us: church, family, community. Traditional values. The backside of our Dodge Neon tells the world the Sullivans are a Trump family.

Politics have made things worse, but Kevin and I were never more than neighbors. Even before Donald Trump. My neighbor is pretty smug and entitled. The man buys a new car every year. His wife looks like she's half made of plastic. Kevin might be a good dad, but his home clearly lacks the Lord's presence. Kevin obviously thinks he's too good to have a relationship with Jesus Christ. And it isn't just church: He was clearly too busy making money to teach that spoiled little dog of theirs not to bark.

The neighborhood was a whole lot better before that obnoxious little dog got here.

Kevin has the size of bank account Kate and I have never had. He has the type of money we could only imagine. The only reason we own a house in this neighborhood is because my grandfather gave each of his grandchildren enough for a small down payment on a home. The man drove a beat-up old beater his entire life, just so he could give us a down payment. I'm proud that my family could pass down something of value to me. I'm proud that my grandfather didn't measure his worth with new cars. Because of the example he set, we have been blessed with a nice home, but we've never, ever had a new car.

In the last two years Kevin has gotten three. One of them is a BMW. Three new cars, and one of them is a Beemer. But underneath all his money, Kevin lacks a moral core.

Just like most liberals.

Marina

I am Mexican the way Bill O'Reilly is Irish.

Meaning, I am genuinely one-quarter Mexican, but with a few exceptions my Spanish is limited to "No queso on the frijoles."

"Por favor."

Out west, where we lived and where I grew up before we moved here for Kevin's job, I wasn't Hispanic at all. Out west no one ever called me a "Latina." I was more often mistaken for being Jewish. It's a stereotype, but my nose is on the bigger end of the spectrum and so are my boobs, so more often than not I was Marina the Jew, not Marina the Latina.

Or I was just Marina, the slightly-tanner-than-normal white girl.

Then we moved to the Midwest, and I was suddenly the darkest person on our street. Not the darkest Hispanic-looking person. The darkest person, period. I stood out. I was noticed. I was watched. It wasn't just my skin tone. It was everything about me. Everything I did became a statement about a culture or an identity that I never asked for and, until we moved here, never really identified with. Then we moved to this part of the country and suddenly, with one label, everyone was both curious about me, while also already knowing all they needed to know.

Big hair? Nice jewelry? Ah yes, that's the Mexican in you. We know because we saw the girls on the Mexican channel when we were in the taco place.

Speaking of tacos, if you're looking for a good recipe, ask Marina.

(I do make good tacos, but I don't make good tacos because I look like I should know how to make good tacos. My mother was horrible in the kitchen. I make good tacos because I taught myself how to cook.)

In the city things are different. There are black people and Jewish people and Bosnian people and Mexicans and people who look different than our neighbors, who I'm pretty sure all come from Germany. Diversity is why I love going into the city. Living in the Midwestern suburbs isn't all bad, though. There are a lot of things I love about our new hometown. Out west, we lived in a tract home cookie-cutter neighborhood for eight years and never knew anyone. One year after we moved here, Kevin's mom committed suicide. Rick and Kate took the kids while we flew back to handle his mom's funeral, and we barely even knew them. That's the type of community we live in.

Don't get me wrong, I am not ashamed of people thinking I'm Mexican or Latina or whatever, and I am technically part-Mexican. My grandfather immigrated to America during the Revolution. He was just a boy when he left Mexico, running through the hills and away from the violence in his hometown toward the border and a better life. Back then, there wasn't much to it. He crossed over, got a job in a band in a nightclub, and eventually met my grandmother. They had my mother later in life.

My grandfather worked hard to assimilate. He eventually owned a hardware store and was elected Mayor of the tiny little town he lived and died in, just over the border. Kevin loves politics. I hate politics. His mother's father is an American-made monster. My mother's father was a mayor. And a business owner. And a volunteer fire chief. And an immigrant. Really, when you think about the differences between our grandfathers, it's like a black fly in your chardonnay.

Or a death row pardon, two minutes too late.

I am proud of my immigrant grandfather. He worked hard to earn a good life in America. He worked hard to become an American. That's why I don't like it when people here in the middle assume I must know how bad immigrants have it. I don't know how bad they have it specifically because my grandfather worked hard to make sure his family and my mom had a good life.

One of my favorite memories is working behind the counter of his hardware store when I was a little girl.

"Mi pequenña estrellita," he would say, his hand on the top of my head, my feet on a milk crate. "Get your education, and one day the store will be yours, mi pequenña señora jefe."

I remember the smell of my grandfather's pipe tobacco mixing with the smell of the free popcorn he let me eat all day. My mother inherited and sold the store after he died, and I never got my education, but I still love the smell of pipe smoke and popcorn. My grandfather almost never spoke Spanish in his home or in his store, except when he spoke it to me: His little star. His little boss lady.

Besides asking for no cheese on my beans, the only Spanish I know is the Spanish my grandfather spoke to me in his hardware store.

I'm not ashamed of my Mexican heritage, and I'm proud of my grandfather. He ran from a revolution toward America. My grandfather was a survivor. But my grandfather came here almost one hundred years ago. His struggle was not my struggle and adopting his struggle would feel like all that time he spent building a hardware store and being the mayor and teaching himself English and earning his place in America would mean nothing. Still, I get the Latina thing all the time, whether I want it or not. Especially with everything happening in the news right now. I've even become the noble, defenseless Latina my husband has to defend in every little Facebook fight he gets into, as though I never had to make my own way in the world.

Our oldest daughter Becky gets the Latina thing, too.

The first year she went to school here, one classmate asked Becky if she was Puerto Rican. She said no. Then he asked if she spoke English. When she said yes, without a trace of an accent, her classmate asked, "Really?"

After that Kevin called Becky "Puerto Rican Becky."

He says it's a joke, but I'm not sure how funny it is. I think it's his way of turning the Latina thing Becky and I have been assigned into one more chip on his shoulder. It's his way of turning our struggle into his struggle. It's one more reason to hit back at a world that has taken its fair share of swings at him and his family.

Puerto Rican Becky. Marina the Mexican.

In the middle no one is quite sure what we are. But because they know we're not completely white, they are completely sure they know all they need to know about us.

They know enough to know that if you need a good enchilada recipe and Marina the Mexican isn't around, all you need to do is ask Puerto Rican Becky.

Kate

To anyone who would listen, Rick says I'm the one who makes it all work. It's true. With a little prayer, I make it all work. I made it all work so Rick could have the career he wanted, a career that made him feel important.

Rick always wanted to be a reporter. He loved his job, but working at the paper kept us poor and taught me how to stretch a dollar. Baby after baby, I made it work. One way we made it work was by making sure I had every baby—after the first, at least—during the summer so I didn't have to take time off from teaching second grade. I can't complain though. We have a good life. We have a dependable, predictable life. I love that about us.

Most days in our lives are like every other day, and I love that.

We get up. We shower. We get ready for work. I make Rick a bowl of cheerios or fried eggs for the girls. We talk about our day. I gossip about the teachers I work with. Rick talks to me about what he's seen on his political shows. The girls, the three that still live here, get on the bus for school. Rick gives me a ride to work in our Dodge Neon. All day long Rick makes the rounds, seeing his clients. He visits office complexes, mental institutions, locally owned hotels, movie theaters. Janitorial supply sales are pretty competitive, so Rick tells me. He does his best, though.

My husband always tries his best. It's who he is. It's one reason I love him so much.

I spend all day bent over, teaching my students to read and say please and thank you and learn how to be decent human beings. After our day is over we come home. We eat dinner. Rick and I watch TV after the girls go to bed. The next day we get up and do it again. We combine the paychecks from selling toilet paper to mental hospitals and teaching little kids to read and we make it work. We've made it work for almost thirty years, and I'm so proud of that.

It sounds boring, but most days it's a beautiful life. It's a beautiful life that we've had to work so hard to earn. I go to bed every night in a safe house, with the only man I've ever loved and kids who love me, too. With a little help from Rick's family, we have a good home. A sturdy home. A home that will last. I live six blocks from my parents, who, thank God, are both still healthy and with us. We go to church every Sunday and thank God for what he's given us. We have good kids, too. Our daughters haven't tried drugs. They haven't fallen in love with the wrong man and gotten pregnant too soon.

The days that are like every other day are the good days. The best days.

Then there are the other days.

In his early twenties Rick was diagnosed as manic depressive with psychotic tendencies. Today his doctor says he's bi-polar. Times change, I guess, and so do the labels we use for people. His diagnosis sounds a lot worse than it is. It's not like my husband is dangerous. But some days Rick wakes up, and it wouldn't matter if we had won the Powerball jackpot. On his bad days he's just empty. He's spent.

"You've lost your mojo," I'll say.

Or, if I think he might have lost his mojo but I'm not sure, I'll ask, "How's your mojo?" He's supposed to score his mojo on a one-to-ten scale.

"Seven," he'll say.

"Liar," I'll respond. "I can see you're a two."

I know his score already, but not because of the number he gives me. I already know by the look on his face. In a good marriage, your person knows the real answer in your pauses. Or the angle you take in bed. Or the way you leave your clothes lying on the floor. Rick is bad about that one. On good days he takes his clothes off and puts them in the hamper.

On bad days there are socks and underwear and jeans leaving a trail from our bedroom door to his side of the bed. On the worst days, Rick usually doesn't even realize he's having a bad day. On the worst days, if I were to ask about his mojo, he would say seventeen. Heck, he would say a hundred. On those days Rick thinks he can do anything. On those days he can take things too far. He picks fights on Facebook and talks too much about politics and what's happening to the country. Or what he thinks is happening to the country.

On the worst days, Rick tells jokes that aren't very funny.

The problem is—and, I was raised not to talk about this stuff—but the problem is I think the meds

Rick uses to balance his up days and his down days can get in the way of intimacy. Sometimes he just can't perform in the bedroom. Sometimes he'll be kneeling over me, looking at my body. It's a body that created everything and everyone he loves most in the world. Still, he just can't get his thing to work.

"Katie, you're so pretty. You're so beautiful. You're so sexy."

He'll repeat that, over and over, like a prayer. I know it's the pills. I know it. I know when he's kneeling over my body on the bed with his soft thing in his hand and tears in his eyes, it's about the worst feeling my husband can have.

Even though the pills get in the way, I know Rick likes Marina. I see him watching her while she smokes and sunbathes on her front porch. Sunbathing might be a decent thing to do in Mexico or California or wherever it is she's from, but out here it isn't. Out here sunbathing on her front porch makes Marina stick out. Her behavior keeps her from having friends in our neighborhood. Out here sunbathing on your porch while you smoke cigarettes tells the neighbors about your decency, or lack of it.

She might be a little bit showy, but I know Marina is pretty. I know Rick sometimes watches her through our window. She's younger. She isn't waking up at 5:00 AM to make fried eggs before she gets dropped off for work in a broken-down Dodge Neon. She can afford facials and skin peels and lip injections and anti-aging creams and a lot of other things that just aren't in our family budget.

It's okay, though.

We've made it through worse than Rick watching the neighbor getting even tanner and darker on her front porch. Surviving on a second-grade teacher's salary and the money Rick made at the local paper while raising four kids toughened us up. It toughened me up, that's for sure. I'll be Marina's friend. Or at least I'll be friendly. I'll even spend time on her porch with her tiny dog, so long as she wears all her clothes. I don't care if she's Mexican or black or Chinese. That stuff doesn't matter to me. It never has. I'll be her friend. And we'll make it through this.

We'll make it through this.

With God's grace, we'll keep having more days that are like every other day.

Chapter Three

Kevin

A college degree didn't come easy to me. I started my education at a community college, and I had no idea how student loans worked. I was too embarrassed to visit the financial aid office, and no one in my family knew how student loans worked, because until I went no one in my family had ever attended college. I assumed I couldn't get a student loan because of a delinquent car payment, so I paid for my undergraduate degree out of pocket. Because of that I was broke all the time. I was so broke that on the weekends I would sneak into Costco and spend all day eating samples. It was either that or the Salvation Army soup kitchen.

Everything I have was earned the hard way. I wasn't just handed a college degree, like Trump. Like Rick. I worked during the day and went to school at night while earning every degree on my wall.

Every uncle and grandfather I ever had spent his life working in a field, in a factory, or on a railroad line, but my family's struggles weren't just economic. My mom committed suicide a year after we moved to this part of the country. She went home on a Friday, turned on the TV, and swallowed a bottle of pills.

Her life ended three months before she turned fifty-six.

Anyone who knew my mom and her story could see this coming for years. It was one of those things where it was not a surprise that it happened, just a surprise that it happened that day.

My dad is still alive, lucky to survive an eight-year meth addiction and make it to an age where he can start collecting a Social Security check. Still, long-term meth use does terrible damage to your brain. I don't need to read a medical journal to know this, I just need to listen to my dad reminisce about sharing a Billy Beer with me. Billy Beer was a beer briefly made by Billy Carter, Jimmy Carter's brother, three years before I was born.

Point being, the blue-collar workers watching the world pass them by, struggling to deal with the addictions and demons that come from seeing a world they thought they knew slip through their hands? Those are the people I was raised by. Those people are my dad, my uncles, my grandfathers. With the exception of my brother Cory, who survived the same shitty childhood I did, they are every man I've ever loved—and some I've hated. They are the people I have worked hard my whole life to leave behind.

Those are my people. They aren't Rick's people. Rick was born into a life of privilege, a life that I could only dream of. My family lived in a tent for a little while, and I know what grilled cheese made with commodity bread and government cheese tastes like. I grew up believing that having Kraft Singles in your fridge was a sign of immeasurable wealth. I had so many poverty-fueled childhood issues related to food that Marina kept purchasing Kraft Singles long after I realized Kraft Singles aren't cheese at all. Those thin, plastic-coated plastic-tasting yellow slices were a sign to me that we were doing okay, that we were making our way in the world. Plastic cheese tells me I've won.

Rick, though?

When my son and I ride our bikes through town, Rick's last name is on street signs. Street signs. Like a president. Rick isn't rich, and yes, I drive a better car than he does—but Rick was born with something I am working incredibly hard to create: a family name that means something. Rick has never had to show anyone he belonged.

Rick was born belonging.

If you're asking me to feel empathy for blue-collar workers in Ohio who've seen their quality of life erode for decades, I can do that. I can understand why blowing up the system, fallout be damned, might be appealing, especially if the alternative is a pipe in your mouth or a needle in your arm. Or a bottle of pills by your bed. I can feel empathy and sympathy for those people. They are my people.

But sympathy for Rick?

Rick, who inherited a family name and probably his home from his parents? Rick, who probably thinks things will always work out for the best because for him—a man with his last name on street signs—they always have? Rick, who has a MAGA bumper sticker on his Dodge Neon? Rick, who posts articles on Facebook that any idiot can see are obviously fake? Rick, who thinks my wife should swim back to Mexico? Rick, who can't see how gross it is to be a Trump fanboy while raising a house full of women? Rick, who pretends like he has it so rough when he has no idea what it's like to wake up to your dad fighting the stranger who's trying to get inside your tent?

      Fuck that.

      Fuck Rick.

Rick

      We had our first kid too young. Not young like those kids in the MTV shows my girls like to watch, but young enough that we were scared. We were twenty-two, four months from graduating college. We had our entire lives ahead of us. Then Kate had my baby in her belly.

      I firmly believe the Lord forbids all forms of sexual deviancy: homosexuality, cross-dressing, tucking your privates back so you can pretend you're a girl. All of it. Including premarital sex. The Lord meant for sex to occur between one man and one woman, within a committed and loving marriage.

Unfortunately, the Lord wasn't there to remind me of that the night we got pregnant the first time.

Who *was* there?

Kate. The most beautiful woman I've ever met. The love of my life. She was in a white tank top and jeans, looking better in an outfit she spent twenty dollars on than a million of Hollywood's prettiest actresses dressed in million-dollar gowns. Truth be told, three decades and four kids hasn't stopped her from looking great in a tank top and jeans. She will always, always be the prettiest, sexiest thing I've ever seen. That's why I hate it when I can't make my willy work for her. I hate the idea that she might think my inability to perform is because I'm not attracted to her.

Nothing could be further from the truth.

It's true, Kate doesn't look like Marina. Then again, I don't have the money to buy my wife new body parts. But I am proud of Katie. I'm proud of the way she looks. I'm proud of the family she's built. I'm proud of the way she serves God. I'm proud of the way she holds me together, even when things feel like they are coming apart and I'm not doing so well.

What am I not proud of?

The way I reacted to finding out about our first baby. I will never, ever let go of the shame I feel about the first thought I had after Kate told me she was pregnant.

Truth be told, I wanted her to have an abortion.

I never said it, but I think she knew. Even then she knew me. She knew every part of my face. She knew every freckle that was already there and every line that would come. Like the Lord, a good wife knows what's in your heart. My fear and lack of faith in myself and the Lord was written all over my face when she told me we would have a baby. Thankfully the Lord said something to her before I could.

She looked up from her bean burrito and told me what He had said to her.

"Rick, we're having a girl," she said.

"Okay," I said, squeezing her hand, letting the girl I loved and Jesus take the lead.

That night in Taco Bell was the real beginning of us. It was the start of our grownup love story. And, like usual, the Lord was right. Kate gave birth to our daughter Anna seven months later. Over the years the Lord would bless us with three more daughters: Kelly, Madison, and Peyton.

Raising four girls on our income hasn't been easy. Not at all. It's kind of funny. Kevin thinks I disagree with him about everything. I don't. I think workers are getting a raw deal, and I wouldn't be opposed to a higher minimum wage. I don't think someone should be paid fifteen dollars an hour to flip burgers, not when some of the teachers who work with Kate have to get summer jobs. But working people deserve a roof over their heads. Years of paying off my baby girl's delivery, like she was our

Dodge Neon, made me know healthcare is broken, but the solution isn't Obama's socialism.

I know Kevin thinks I'm some sort of whack-job fanatic. He always has. You can see it in his eyes when we talk in the street. He's trying to get away from me as soon as he possibly can.

If Kevin would get a beer with me, maybe he would see that I'm no lunatic. I am not a fanatic. Politically, there are two things I care deeply about. The Lord told Kate she would have our little girl. The Lord forgave Kate and me for our premarital sin. The Lord wanted me to be a dad, and when He saw me waiver, He intervened. The Lord has blessed the marriage and the kids that came after that night in Taco Bell. The Lord guided me both times I lost my job. I cannot argue with the Lord, and the Lord has told my church that abortion is wrong. It's a transgression.

Like usual, He's right.

Even though he's a liberal, Kevin is a good dad. I can see he and his wife have done a good job raising those kids. But Hitler could have been a good dad too, if he had had the chance. Can't you see Hitler, bent over playing cops and robbers, right before he ordered the murder of millions of innocent babies? I can. If I close my eyes I can see it. I can see Hitler playing. I can see him smiling beneath that weird little mustache. If I close my eyes I can see Kevin with that same mustache.

That probably sounds crazy, but I'm no fanatic.

I'm just Rick. I used to be a reporter for a tiny little local newspaper. Then my paper went out of business. Now I sell janitorial supplies. I'm just one of the millions of people getting chewed up and spit out by a world that's supposed to be changing for the better. Besides abortion, the other thing I care about is illegals.

We live in a country of laws. We have rules and borders that have to be respected. Even Obama said so himself. My family came from Germany. So did Kate's family. Right through Ellis Island. They came the right way. I'm not saying Mexicans shouldn't come here, but if they do, they need to come the right way. President Trump doesn't hate Mexicans. He doesn't. He just believes you need to do things the right way.

Like me. Like my family.

Chapter Four

Kevin

Until my early twenties, the fanciest restaurant I ever ate at was a Golden Corral, and that only happened twice: once to celebrate the time my mom bought a used Pontiac Grand Am, and again when my dad was promoted to shift supervisor. A Pontiac Grand Am, though not a used one, had always been my mom's dream car. Brand new cars weren't a thing my family did, though. Mostly because they couldn't afford new cars, but also because my parents were people who long ago realized the futility of believing in a reach that extended one's grasp, and they struggled to dream brand new dreams.

We celebrated my mom's Grand Am before Golden Corral was exclusively a buffet. That was back when it was a sit-down restaurant. It wasn't good steak, and I was a college graduate before I learned steak could be ordered any way other than well-done, with ketchup. Now, when traveling to meet clients, I go to restaurants where the waiters never write anything down, the water is served at room temperature, and the burgers are served with a "pureed tomato paste with a hint of garlic, ground pepper, and a complex mix of fresh herbs grown in our garden."

Which, for the record, is actually just ketchup.

In the restaurants I eat in now, no one would ever (EVER) put ketchup on steak, and BLTs come "deconstructed." What does it mean when a BLT is deconstructed? It means the food is arranged so that it doesn't resemble in any way what the dish is supposed to be. It might taste okay, but pork belly next to kale next to a cup of aioli next to an artisanal cracker is *not* a BLT.

I thought of that word "deconstructed" the last year we attended Rick's backyard "Fall Harvest" party. These parties always began the same way. Marina, the kids and I would awkwardly stand alone in a lonely corner of Rick's backyard, not knowing a single member of Rick's extended family or anyone from his church. We would continue to stand around until Rick came up, slapped me on the back, and started talking baseball. Kate would take the peanut butter eyeballs from Marina, and we would all spend the next two hours trying to blend in a with a group of people we had nothing in common with.

I was always ecstatic when the whole awkward experience ended.

The last year we attended Rick's party was 2015. Like clockwork, a few minutes after we arrived Rick came up, slapped me on the back, handed me a hotdog, and started asking me how I thought the team's starting pitching looked for next year. By then, after three years of Rick's fake Halloween parties, my neighbor knew how I liked my hotdogs: ketchup. Regular ketchup, without a complex mix of fresh herbs. No mustard, no relish, just ketchup.

I know some people consider ketchup on a hotdog only slightly less trashy than ketchup on a steak. What can I say, though? Some things are hard to shake, no matter how hard you try. I liked my ketchup, and Rick knew it—and, to his credit, judging someone for what they put on their food is not his thing. Mexicans might be feral animals, the minimum wage might be the devil's plot to destroy the God-fearing capitalists Rick worshipped, and women might best belong in the kitchen—but the man did not judge me for what I put on my hotdogs.

I am reluctant to give a Nazi any praise at all, but Rick didn't judge a man for liking ketchup. What Rick didn't know was that choking down a cheap, boiled hotdog was about as appealing to me as the government grilled cheeses I ate as a kid. Every year I ate those hotdogs to be neighborly, but that last year I just couldn't do it. That year the hotdog on my bun had spent too long at the bottom of the hotdog water and was extra mushy. "Extra mushy" is no one's idea of a good hotdog.

"Rick," I said, "this hotdog looks deconstructed."

He just stood there, looking back and forth between me and a boiled, ketchup soaked, mushy hotdog.

"Yeah," he said. "Hey, Carpenter had a heck of a year, right?"

It took me a moment to realize he was talking about a baseball player, not a literal carpenter.

"Yeah, right? Great year. Great year," I said.

I wondered if Rick could tell that I had no idea who Carpenter was. I wasn't the only confused person in this conversation. I could tell Rick had never heard the word deconstructed before in his life, at least as it related to food. I should have known. It wasn't a money thing—Rick just didn't eat in places where they deconstructed a BLT.

I had introduced something new and foreign to Rick's vocabulary, and I could tell he didn't appreciate it. I didn't mean to hurt his feelings. I didn't mean to sound like a pretentious douchebag. I'm not pretentious. It is impossible for someone like me to be pretentious. I grew up thinking a well-done steak at Golden Corral was the fanciest meal you could eat to celebrate the purchase of a brand-new used Grand Am. For much of my childhood, my family survived on food stamps. My parents even pretended to be separated so we could qualify for additional help from the state.

It is literally impossible for people who grew up eating Hamburger Helper bought with food stamps to become pretentious.

I just couldn't eat Rick's boiled hotdogs anymore. I wasn't judging him for his food choices, either. In fact, back then, I didn't judge him at all. I'm not a judgmental person. I had just gotten back from a trip to Maine to see the fall colors with Marina, where we spent three nights by the ocean and ate nothing but lobster rolls and clam chowder. I was just trying to be a little better.

I was trying to be a little classier than ketchup and mushy, boiled hotdogs.

Rick

Lord willing, you make it work. You never buy a "new" new car. Hopefully you can find something with less than a hundred thousand miles on the odometer, though that's not likely. Hopefully the engine starts, and the AC blows cold. Your daughters share hand-me-downs and hand-me-ups. Your wife becomes a coupon ninja, and you know part of the money she saves goes back to her classroom to help some future felon from the ghetto whose parents (usually parent, with no "s") spend all their government money and food stamps on beer and Snickers and fried chicken, rather than a box of Kleenex for their kid.

You never, ever go to movies. Unless it's the dollar theater, and even then you don't go often because your feet stick to the floor and your daughters complain about what might be on the dollar theater movie seats.

Everyone gets a job at fourteen. Everyone.

Before that, every girl in the house learns how to babysit—for the family, and for other families. Nickels, dimes, quarters, and pennies are picked up and placed in jars and saved for birthday parties. The change in the jar piles up and once or twice a year you can take your wife out for a steak at Applebee's. Your girls' birthday parties always have homemade cakes. Your girls' prom dresses are always homemade. So are their Fall Harvest costumes. One year your wife takes an empty box, paints it to look like the Yellow Pages, and your oldest daughter wins a prize for a costume made from garbage your wife found behind the grocery store. Of course, this happened back when there were still phonebooks. And newspapers. And common sense.

Food is always the biggest expense. Yes, we raised girls, but girls still eat. Especially teenage girls. Because they never seem to stop eating, your wife buys everything in bulk. Every bulk item she buys is generic. Your girls think fruit snacks, generic or not, are a delicacy only rich kids can afford. You and your wife worry that kids who associate fruit snacks with rich people will grow up with a chip on their shoulder that will never leave.

Your wife learns to get creative with Hamburger Helper. All-beef hotdogs? For a party where we have to feed more than a hundred family members and church friends?

No way.

Your wife buys hotdogs in bulk. Just like she buys everything else. She buys hotdogs made from a combination of meats, most likely pig hooves and that dangly thing that hangs from a chicken's neck. But the Lord has blessed you with a big family. The Lord has blessed you with a family that isn't rich but is part of the fabric of your community. Your Fall Harvest party is full. You are so busy saying hello to second- and third-cousins that you don't have time to grill your chicken neck hotdogs.

You stick them in a boiler full of water and move on.

"Rick," your uncle says, grabbing you in a bear hug. "Carpenter had a heck of a year, right?"

"Heck of a year," you say. "Heck of a year."

You're just happy to spend a nice fall afternoon talking to people you love about the things you love. You don't care about what the hotdogs are made from, or how much they cost. How much your hotdogs cost says nothing about you. You say hello to a neighbor you've known since the two of you were on the same little league team.

Sometimes the pig hoof and chicken neck hotdogs get a little soft from sitting at the bottom of the boiler. Sometimes they get destructed, or whatever it was Kevin said. That's okay, though. Because you had a lot of kids, and you aren't some flashy marketing consultant with a brand-new Beemer. You can't afford GMO gluten-free hotdogs, or whatever it is the Harrison family eats. You lost the career you loved, and now you sell toilet cleaning supplies to mental institutions. It's nothing fancy, but you've made it work. No matter what the neighbors think of you or your hotdogs, you'll make it work. You and your wife will make it work. Lord willing.

Marina

Kevin's story begins with a mother who had a truly horrific father and a nightmare childhood.

From there the story skips ahead a bit, to Kevin's own childhood poverty, where, if you listen to him, he survives on nothing more than government grilled cheese and the hope for a better life. I have never heard any human make so many references to government cheese. Really, I never heard a single reference to government cheese until I met Kevin. His childhood horror story continues into his early adulthood, when his mom discovered OxyContin and his dad got hooked on crystal meth. At some unknown point in the future, the story concludes with Kevin redeeming himself and his entire family and making our last name something special.

That's a big thing for Kevin. He wants our family name to mean something more than meth and OxyContin and government cheese.

The thing is, I don't really become part of the story until Kevin and I meet. I know he knows I have a story, but I don't know if he really knows I existed separately and apart from him before our stories merged.

What's my story?

I guess the most important part of my story is that Kevin isn't my first husband. I got pregnant with Becky when I was eighteen. My first husband was a little older, but that wasn't even the biggest problem. The biggest problem was that he was through and through a shithead. A shithead to the core. A deadbeat dad in the making from the moment I got pregnant. I could see it in his eyes. But, my parents gave me an ultimatum: marry the shithead or forget I ever knew them.

"It is," my father said, "what God wants."

"Your God can go straight to hell," I wanted to say, but didn't.

I looked to my mother, who simply said, "We raised you better than this. We raised you to be a good Christian woman."

It wasn't the last time I was in a church, but right there and then my relationship with my parents' God ended.

Forcing your child to marry her baby's father under threat of abandonment by God and her family is not exactly the best foundation for a marriage, and my relationship with the shithead ended not long after it started. I just couldn't do it. Me and the baby girl that would grow up to be Puerto Rican Becky were out. Done. We bounced.

We were two kids who also happened to be mother and daughter. For the next three years, I waitressed, went to beauty school, dated, and was a mom. We were two girls, too young to be mother and daughter, making our own way, but we did okay.

We were survivors.

Every week we would collect our spare change and walk across the street to a gas station with a Taco Bell in it. We would split a bag of Cheetos and a dollar menu bean burrito, and spend hours laughing and eating before we went home to our dumpy little apartment. If I tell that story now it feels sad, but I know when I'm old, and when Becky is old, we'll think of a bean burrito coated in Cheeto dust and smile.

That was my story.

I was a girl who grew up with a little money from the sale of a hardware store her mom inherited after her Grandpa died. I grew up a girl who was supposed to be eternally forgiven by Jesus, but instead made an unforgivable mistake and got pregnant by a shithead. I became a woman who learned to make my own way, the mother of an amazing little girl with a bean-and-Cheeto-dust covered face that could make me forget every bad thing in my life, including the shithead. She even made me thankful for the shithead.

Then everything changed.

I met Kevin one night in a dirty, smoke-filled little bar after I had gotten off my shift waitressing.

We were both twenty-two, and I noticed him immediately. It was hard not to. He had a tight t-shirt on and a copy of *Tortilla Flats* in his back pocket. He seemed complete. I wasn't complete, but Kevin didn't know that. He followed me around the bar until I had no choice but to talk to him.

I took his phone, a little flip phone, and put my name in the phone book. And that's when our stories merged.

Three months later Kevin was my husband, and sometime during our first six months as husband and wife he became Becky's dad. He couldn't adopt her right away (the shithead still insisted on being the shithead) but he was her dad in a real and special way that was better than any court document. He decided he was going to be her dad, and he made it happen. I will always love Kevin for that. I will love him for never seeing me as damaged goods. I love him for loving Becky like she was someone he had lost in another life and then found in this one.

I will always love him for being such an amazing dad to Becky, and to our other two kids, Kevin Jr. and Eliza.

Kevin wove Becky and me into his story. He was hard luck. We were hard luck. He rescued us in a real way, and he also rescued us in his story. It's a story he's superimposed on all of our lives. That's what he does. Kevin rescues people, especially people like us. He's a defender of the downtrodden, a rescuer of women who need to be rescued. It's who he is.

That's his story, and he wrote me and Becky into that story.

Kate

I didn't think of Rick as handsome when we met.

Mostly because we were ten years old and he was still enough of a little kid to wear *Dukes of Hazard* t-shirts and play with toys. By the time he was fourteen things were different. I was wild about him. He was so tall and confident and good looking that I never really looked at anyone else. Ever. Rick is the only man I've ever wanted. It took a while for him to see me the same way, but by the time we were sixteen, we were practically one person. RickandKate. One word for the rest of our lives, from junior prom to today.

RickandKate.

One word. Forever.

We went to the prom and had our pictures taken, Rick with his mullet and mustache, me with big bangs that were stiff and flammable with hairspray. It was a miracle that someone didn't accidently light my hair on fire with a cigarette that night.

Our girls laugh at those pictures now and wonder how we could have possibly been attracted to each other, but we were. I have been crazy about that mustache ever since it started sprouting on Rick's upper lip. It would be years before RickandKate slept together, but that night at the prom was better than making love. I remember my hand on his neck and his hand on my hip. I remember how his stubble scratched my chin, how his wispy mustache tickled my upper lip. I remember that old eighties song "Need You Tonight" playing as we danced, moving near each other, our bodies lightly touching.

"Katie, you remind me of the ocean," he whispered, his mustache brushing my ear. It was such a romantic thing to say. Me and Rick have never been to the ocean. I reminded him of something he could only imagine.

I hope I'm still as good as something he can only imagine. No matter what the girls think of our hair and shoulder pads and ill-fitting tuxes and dresses, we were so attracted to each other back then.

Are, I mean.

We are so attracted to each other.

Chapter Five

Kevin

The weekend of the *Access Hollywood* video was a rough one in our house. I misread how Marina would react to it. To me, the footage CNN aired that entire weekend was nothing but good news. I welcomed the video because it made me believe that a man who had always been vastly unfit for the presidency saw his chances of occupying the White House go from slim to none. It gave me hope. A taped confession of non-consensual pussy grabbing came as a relief. There was simply no way he would win.

I even took our family out for a celebratory dinner at Ikea.

"Can I get an extra side of mac n' cheese?" my son, Kevin Jr. asked while we were waiting to get our Swedish meatballs.

"You can get two extra sides of mac n' cheese," I said.

That night our table was crammed with little plates of mac n' cheese. How else do you celebrate a recording of a presidential candidate talking about sexual assault? I also bought a chair we didn't need, just to further mark the occasion. Marina is right when she says I am a bit of a spender, that I like to deal with my issues by buying things I don't need.

There's a reason for that.

Every purchase my family ever made was planned out for months, and often required using layaway. With layaway you went to Kmart and picked a winter coat in the heat of July and paid for it in four installments.

I've worked hard to make sure my kids have a better life. We don't buy winter coats at Kmart, and we don't use layaway. I've earned the life I live and the money I spend. I've made occasional spontaneous purchases: an electric bicycle, an old Jeep, a new Jeep when I got tired of the old Jeep, a new truck when I got tired of the new jeep, and a new BMW for Marina. Substantial purchases, no doubt, but not exactly speed boats and gold-laced curtains. I live like I'm upper-middle class, not like I'm Scarface.

What I celebrated that weekend—the likely end of a candidate who could only run for president because of his daddy's name and his daddy's money—reminded my wife of every man who tried to take something that wasn't his to take. That weekend I talked about sexual assault and its impact on the presidential race so much that I became just like every other guy I detested: self-consumed and secure in the fact that it would never be me getting assaulted. I talked like the video was just a matter of politics, in some ways no different than the voting habits of thirty-five-year-old soccer moms in Hamilton County, Ohio.

Except it was different.

The more I talked, the worse it got. I was sure we were headed toward a fight, the sort of epic battle that can only occur between a husband and wife. On its surface, the battle appears to be about one thing (a cretin running for President) when it is actually about something else (a cretin who hasn't realized that a presidential candidate talking about sexual assault is nothing to celebrate.)

Thankfully, Rick made sure the battle never happened.

"Did you see this?" Marina asked, handing me her phone.

"What the fuck? Seriously?"

I was looking at one of the longest Facebook posts I had ever read.

"Oh my God," she said, as she continued reading alongside me. "How long is this thing?"

As Marina read, her eyes started welling up with tears.

"What the fuck," I said, as I finished a Facebook post that was more like a blog than a status update. "Seriously?"

What the fuck. Seriously? That's what you say when you see a five-hundred-word rant from your neighbor comparing Bill Clinton to Donald Trump, mixed in with a few graphic examples of "locker room talk" your neighbor claims to have heard. It was strange that Rick thought the world was just waiting to hear his opinion about the election. The post was also strange because I couldn't remember hearing Rick swear or use vulgar language.

Truthfully though, we hardly ever spoke. Rick could have the vocabulary of a truck driver, for all I knew. Rick's social media profile was an outlier for me. I had long ago unfollowed or blocked the most rabid pro-Trump members of my family, which was relatively easy to do. It had been ten years since I had seen any of my Trump-loving uncles and cousins, and I'm sure if they thought about me unfollowing or blocking them at all it came with a sense of relief. They wouldn't have to hear me rant about gun control, and I wouldn't have to see memes about killing all the Muslims and letting Allah sort it out. It was what we in the consulting game call a win-win.

Rick is different, though. To begin with, he lives across the street. He isn't like my uncles and cousins. I couldn't just completely forget about him, try as I might. Even though each of us couldn't stomach what the other stood for, we still raised our hands in a wave toward each other. My job gives me precious little time with my family, and it's always been that way, so I don't mow my own lawn—but Rick does. No matter how bad or ugly the campaign got, he would always raise his hand from his old-fashioned push mower in a neighborly wave, and I always raised mine back.

Until that day.

That Sunday morning began with my wife opening Facebook and bursting into tears. The fact that her neighbor—a man she made her famous bloody peanut butter eyeballs for—could be so callous about a rapist running for President was just too much. In her tears I saw my chance. I saw the chance to redeem myself. I saw a chance to stick up for her. I saw a chance to avoid a fight that had been stirring for at least two days, if not for the months leading up to that, when all I could talk about was Donald Trump.

Rick

Can someone please explain to me the difference between Bill Clinton and Donald Trump? How does one guy sexually harass women for years, and only get more popular because of it, while one guy uses a little locker room talk and is suddenly a monster?

I'm not trying to pick a political fight. I just really don't understand the double standard. I would never talk about my women the way Trump talks about his. My father taught me better than that. I would never attack someone or grab them or even talk about grabbing them. But I would also never cheat on Kate with an intern. I would never have affair after affair and lie about it. If you asked me if oral sex with a woman who isn't Kate is cheating, I would never ask you what "is" is.

I just don't understand the double standard. That's all I was trying to say. Did I say it as good as I could have?

Probably not.

Did I say it as good as Kevin would have?

No, I didn't. Then again, I stopped writing for a living when the paper went out of business. Kevin is a marketing consultant, whatever that is. I'm pretty sure it involves him knowing how to make a bunch of bullpucky sound like the truth. I am absolutely positive making up bullpucky pays well. The same weekend I got the message from Kevin, I saw him unloading a brand-new chair from his brand-new truck.

I wasn't trying to offend him or his wife. In his Facebook message, Kevin made it sound like he was protecting Marina from me, as though comparing Bill Clinton and Donald Trump was all the evidence he needed to brand me a threat to women everywhere.

He should know better. Every one of my girls adores me. In our house our daughters learned three things: respect for the Lord and their father, respect for their family, and respect for themselves. We didn't raise the type of girls who would ever let someone grab their private parts without their permission, even if it was Donald Trump or Bill Clinton or some other rich and famous guy doing the grabbing.

I serve the Lord. I'm not a sexist. I'm not a rapist. I just don't understand the double standards in our country anymore. That was all I was trying to say.

Kevin

Rick,

I just wanted to let you know that I've made the decision to block you. It's not because I hate you. It's because our views are so different than yours that I just think we can't be Facebook friends. I appreciate that your politics are different than mine, and that you have a different set of values. However, if we are to remain neighborly, I just can't have my family and especially my wife exposed to the sexism and racism I see in your feed. I like you as a neighbor and respect you as a father and would rather not end up as enemies—but your words do have an impact, and this morning they've hurt the person I love the most. I can't have my wife in tears, believing that a monster lives across the street.

I hope you'll understand, and that after this election is over things can return to normal. Until then I think it's best if we remain neighbors rather than Facebook friends.

Thank you,

Kevin

Copy. Paste. Send.

While I was at it, I logged in to Marina's profile and blocked Rick for her, too.

Rick

Dear Kevin,

Let me get this straight: Clinton rapes Juanita Broderick and screws a twenty-year-old girl with a cigar in the White House, and Trump is the bad guy. How hypocritical can you possibly be? This isn't Trump running against Mother Theresa. Hillary defended Bill and destroyed those women. You can't see the hypocrisy here?

And monster across the street? What's that supposed to mean?

Your neighbor, only.

Rick.

Delete.

Dear Kevin,

Really? You're going to block me and lecture me over this? Didn't Kate and me take your kids when your mom killed herself, and now that's just forgotten? You love Hillary and I support Trump and now it's just the heck with you

Rick? Why is that? Is it because I have a mental illness? Is that it? I thought you progressives were all about tolerance. Guess not.

And what did you mean by a "monster" across the street?

Rick

PS When someone else in your family kills them self you need to find a different neighbor to take care of them. Don't come crawling to me and Kate again. Maybe you're the monster.

Delete.

Dear Kevin,

Fuck you, you sanctimonious prick. I'm more than happy you don't want to be Facebook friends anymore. Good luck with the rest of eighth grade. Asshole. Your friend? No, your neighbor.

Sincerely,

The Monster Across the Street

Delete.

I don't curse that often. I read the Bible every day. It's almost impossible for someone like me to be profane, but sometimes my anger gets the best of me.

Plus, it wouldn't have mattered what I said. Kevin blocked me, so I couldn't reply to his message. I guess there's no way to reach a person who's decided they don't want to hear what you have to say anymore.

Monster across the street? There are no monsters on this street. That's why my family helped us buy this home. That's why we live in this place.

There are no monsters here.

Chapter Six

Kevin

IN THIS HOUSE WE BELIEVE
HEALTHCARE IS A HUMAN RIGHT
BLACK LIVES MATTER
WOMEN'S RIGHTS ARE HUMAN RIGHTS
NO HUMAN IS ILLEGAL
SCIENCE IS REAL
LOVE IS LOVE

America might be losing its mind, but it is important to me that my neighborhood knows what our family stands for. That's why I ordered our tolerance sign and went to Home Depot to buy a stake and some nails. I don't know where we keep tools in our house, so sometimes it's just easier to buy them new. I don't go to Home Depot often. Correction: I don't go to Home Depot ever. That's why it felt so good to buy the nails, get a stake, and use them to drive the sign I bought off Etsy into the ground.

I was pushing myself out of my comfort zone to let our neighbors know exactly what we believe.

The first day the sign was up, a car stopped at the curb in front of our house. It was one of our neighbors from four or five houses down. I was sure we were going to have a confrontation, sure that my driveway basketball game with Kevin, Jr. was going to be interrupted by our neighbor telling us why some human beings are in fact illegal, so long as they're brown.

"I like your sign," the neighbor said after rolling down her window. She was in her sixties, grey-haired, and looked vaguely familiar. I didn't know her name and was too embarrassed to ask. She was my neighbor and I didn't know her, and it seemed too late to admit that.

"Thank you," I said, "I appreciate it."

After a pause I followed with, "We need to stick together."

There was no response to that, just a small wave before she pushed the button to roll her window up.

Our sign is a little thing, but it matters to me that the neighborhood knows we're an island of tolerance in an ocean of hate. In our house it doesn't matter if you're gay, Muslim, or Mexican. Labels do not matter in our house. Plus, I won't lie. It gave me satisfaction to catch Rick staring at the sign from behind his living room window. It gave me pleasure to know that our sign would be a daily reminder that not everyone reads Breitbart, not everyone thinks Donald Trump was anointed by God, not everyone hates brown people.

From behind his window I saw his discomfort and anger at the realization that not every liberal lived in San Francisco and waited until forty-five to have kids. Some liberals, at least in Rick's neighborhood, were parents too. Some liberals were normal, or at least normal by Rick's standards. We drove trucks. We worked regular jobs. We put our pants on one leg at a time. There were liberals in Rick's neighborhood who worked for the life they had and didn't just order up that life on their Obama cell phone and pay for it with a WIC card.

The sign told Rick that conservatives don't have a lock on family values.

By the time I was twenty-seven, Marina and I were raising three kids on one income. Marina learned how to be creative with tofu and Hamburger Helper and learned how to work her mom's group clothing exchange so our kids got what they needed. We did that, we struggled, we built our family, we went to story time and parent-teacher conferences and managed to raise three kids without making excuses, asking for God's help, or blaming our problems on Mexicans and Muslims.

I wanted to walk up to his door and point to the sign while Marina and the kids stood next to it. I wanted to point to my liberal, part-Mexican family and ask him, "How's that for family values, Rick?" I wanted to watch him struggle to understand someone who didn't fit into his notion of how the world should work. I like to think Rick realized at least some of that when Marina and I put up the sign.

That's why he couldn't look away. That's why he watched us the whole time, staring at us through the window that faces our yard.

Rick

I could care less what Kevin puts in his yard. If he wants to let the neighborhood know he's a socialist, that's fine. If he wants to let the neighborhood know he loves the terrorists in Black Lives Matter, more power to him. For all I care, he can run through the mall with those freaks. He can think that somehow screaming at the employees working at the Dairy Queen in the food court will fix all the race problems Obama caused. Put a machine gun around the guy's neck, and Kevin is practically a Black Panther. One with the struggle and all that.

Give me a break.

If Rick wants to let the neighborhood know that he doesn't care about borders, that's his deal. His wife is Mexican, so he's not telling anyone anything they don't already know. Putting up that sign is his right. Lord willing, this is still America. In America you can put whatever sign you want in your yard. Our government can't stop you from looking like an idiot. At least not yet.

In some places the homeowners' association will keep the neighbors in line, but we don't have one in this neighborhood. We never needed one. Now that the neighborhood is changing, we might have to take another look at that.

It wasn't the sign that got to me. I knew Kevin was liberal from the moment I saw his expensive haircut and "Coexist" bumper sticker. What bothered me was his yard. It wasn't that it was trashy. It was perfect. It was perfect because Kevin didn't do any of the work himself. I asked Kate after I watched him and Marina put that sign up, "What sort of man pays another man to mow his yard?"

"A man who can afford to," Kate said.

"What's that supposed to mean?"

"Nothing. It doesn't mean anything. It just means that if we ever have the money, I don't want to see you pushing that old mower around the yard," she said, kissing me on the cheek. She looked so pretty in her jeans and t-shirt. Just a regular woman, making regular look beautiful. Like always.

"I'll pay another man to take care of my house? No. In this house we mow our own yard."

"Why do you care so much about their yard?"

"I don't care."

"Sounds like you do care. Is this about the yard? Or is it about Marina? Is it her you're looking at?"

The tone was joking, but I knew she was paying close attention to my answer. The wrong answer—even the wrong pause before an answer—can send a fight like this spiraling out of control.

"Seriously? No. It isn't Marina. You know I don't have a thing for Mexican girls."

"Who *do* you have a thing for?"

We were flirting now. I heard it in her voice. We had walked back from the edge of an abyss. "You, Katie. You and only you. In fact, other women make my eyes hurt. They make my willy curl up and hibernate, like a little baby bear."

"Rick!"

Marina? A Mexican girl? Not to be racist, but they just aren't my thing.

Kevin

We were lying in bed, Marina's body pushed against mine, the two of us spooning. It was how we had fallen to sleep for fifteen years. When I'm on the road, it's almost impossible to fall asleep without the cigarettes-and-shampoo smell of her hair in my face. That smell is a perfect smell to me.

"I think he's obsessed with you," I said.

"Who?" she asked.

"Rick."

"Oh honey, lots of guys are obsessed with me," she said, wiggling her butt to tell me she was joking, and maybe even coming on to me.

"Not that way."

"What way then?"

"Because you're Mexican. And he hates Mexicans. Didn't you see his post a couple months back about illegals?"

"First of all, read your own sign. Don't call them illegals. Second of all, illegals and Mexicans are not the same thing. Third of all, will you quit with the Mexican thing? It's bad enough I have to get it from the neighbors."

There it was. The shift from a discussion to a fight. When you've been married long enough, you feel the shift before you hear it. Like lightning and thunder. Her butt quickly moved away from my lap.

"What do you mean the Mexican thing?" I asked.

"I mean you becoming the great defender of Mexicans. I mean you making me part of your fight. I don't feel like your wife. I'm not some Facebook post to argue about. I'm me. Please stop making me your token Mexican to fight with Rick about."

"So you don't care about what's happening in the world?"

"Seriously? Fuck you for saying that. You have no idea what it's like. Do you know every time someone says something about Trump and his stupid fucking wall everyone looks at me? Oh, what does Marina the Mexican think? Is she one of us or one of them? That's fine. I get it. But this is my home. Can't

I just be Marina, here, in this place? Can't I just be me, or do I have to be The Mexican here, too?"

"You're *my* Mexican," I said, trying to get back to flirting. Marina wasn't taking the bait.

"Go."

"Go?"

"Go."

I spent the night on the couch.

Rick

There are only a few things worse than sitting on your couch at 3:00 AM, wide awake after failing to satisfy your wife. Again. One of those is sitting on your couch, looking out your window and realizing your neighbor is up at 3:00 AM. And he's staring at you.

Like some kind of maniac.

Kevin

Seriously, what the fuck is he staring at? Lunatic.

Chapter Seven

Kevin

"Democrats," my dad said, "are for people like us."

It was the fall of 1988. Our family was watching a Dukakis/Bush debate on a little black-and-white TV powered by a generator. We were living in a KOA campground just outside of town. Even at seven years old I didn't have to ask what my dad meant by "people like us."

He meant people who lived in tents. He meant people who still owned a black-and-white TV and used a generator to power it. He meant people who got their peanut butter, bread, eggs, milk, and cheese from the county, rather than the grocery store. He meant people who bought their winter coats in July using Kmart's layaway. He meant people who can only afford used cars. He meant people like my family, people like him, people like the me I would have become if I hadn't gone to college and gotten an education.

At the time my dad was recovering from a broken back. He had been a water well-driller before rupturing several discs lifting a heavy pipe. After the accident he couldn't work for five years. My mom, who only had her GED, took up the slack when my dad got hurt. She supported our family by working at a Burger King and delivering newspapers. When I was a child, my mom's hair always smelled like French fry grease, and her fingers were permanently stained black with newspaper ink. No matter how hard I work to be different than her, I will always respect what my mom did to keep food on our table when my dad was out of a job.

Every Sunday morning, just before dawn, she would lay the seat down in the back of her beat-up S10 Blazer and tuck me and my brother in between stacks of the Sunday paper. I would read that paper, cover to cover, in the early morning light while my mom drove around delivering the Sunday news and listening to George Strait.

I learned about something called "Iran-Contra" to the sound of "Amarillo by Morning."

My parents were rednecks. For a while we lived in a tent. But we weren't stupid, we weren't ignorant, and we were aware that our family's poverty was the result of personal decisions, bad luck, and politics. When Ronald Reagan talked about welfare queens, my parents knew he was talking about them.

We knew politics was more than just a sideshow, which was why my dad fired up the generator and used precious, expensive gas to watch Michael Dukakis, of all people. Of course, Dukakis lost. Badly. People in the eighties loved trickle-down economics, and in 1988 all they wanted was more of

Reagan's ideas—even if they couldn't have more of the man. Reagan must have been good for someone, but I know trickle-down economics never trickled down on my family.

Four years later, things were different. My parents loved the Clintons. Bill Clinton hated the Vietnam War and liked weed and women with big hair. My dad didn't even know where or what Yale was, but he knew where to find weed and women with big hair. Hillary Clinton was a working woman, just like my mom. My parents believed the Clintons weren't just for people like us. When you stripped away the Ivy League law degrees and the expensive haircuts, they were people like us.

They were our people.

Poverty isolates. Or, at least it isolated my family. My parents weren't social. They were awkward and kept to themselves. They didn't have friends. Our family was its own little universe. Letting people in meant letting the world see just how desperate and angry you really were.

The night Bill Clinton was elected in 1992 was the only time I ever remember my parents attending a party. My mom—who gave up drinking in the '70s, right around the time she quit cocaine—had a couple of glasses of wine to celebrate. She even tried sushi. I remember she came home around midnight and went straight to the bathroom, throwing up everything she had eaten. Even though the expensive wine and sushi made her sick, I like to think she fell asleep and woke up the next morning, confident that America was a better place for people like us.

Rick

Are the Sullivans rich? No.

Are the Sullivans a big family? Yes.

My dad has seven brothers and sisters, and my mom has five brothers. When your family has lived in the same place for more than one hundred and twenty years and has that many babies, their name, your name, is going to end up all over town. Some cousin is going to start an HVAC company. A nephew's daughter is going to buy a salon. Lord willing, someone will be the quarterback or point guard for the state champs. Someone will get elected County Judge. Given enough time, your last name will be everywhere.

It's not white privilege. I'm sure the same thing happens in black towns. Given enough time, someone will make a name for your family.

My ancestors made a name for our family. But that wasn't because of money. My great-uncle died on Omaha Beach. That scene in the beginning of *Saving Private Ryan*, the one where soldiers are getting mowed down and blood and limbs are flying all over the place? My great-uncle was one of the men who died in that battle. My great-uncle was one of those heroes.

He and my grandfather were close. My grandfather wore his brother's dog tags for sixty-four years. My father wears them now. One day I hope to wear them, and when I'm gone, one of my nephews will wear them. Long after the letters on those tags are rubbed away, my great-uncle and his sacrifice will stay close to our hearts.

Like I said, we aren't rich. But there are some things you inherit by being a Sullivan. An understanding that you will go to college. A feeling of being part of a community. And, if you're lucky enough, you might inherit a pair of worn and long-faded dog tags that tell the world how much your family has sacrificed for our country. I wanted to serve in the military too. I wanted to earn a set of dog tags that I could pass down to my sons. The Lord works in mysterious ways though, and I never had any sons to pass dog tags down to. That, and my diagnosis got me rejected.

No dog tags for me, unless I inherit them.

I'm patriotic though. I believe in respecting the flag. I believe in respecting my President, as long as that President serves the Lord. I believe in respecting the military. We don't kneel for the national anthem in this house. I don't know what I would do if I saw one of my daughters take a knee before a softball game. Lord willing, they were raised better than that. I wasn't there for it, but I believe my community didn't hesitate for a second when it decided to name that street after my great-uncle. My values are my community's values. They are good values.

Live your life in service of the Lord. Respect your country. Work hard and don't take a handout.

It doesn't matter whether you're black, Mexican, or Chinese. In America, if you live by these values, you will get ahead. If blacks really wanted to make something of themselves, they would drop their signs, get a job, and get down on their knees for prayer and get up off their knees when our anthem is played. Just like I do. No one lets me take a knee. No one gives me a handout.

If Marina's people want to make it here, they need to get in line and do it right. Just like my ancestors did.

That's all I'm saying.

These are good values. They don't need to change. They were the values that built my town and my country. We don't need to throw out our values and the Lord just because it's politically correct to do so. My political beliefs have nothing to do with racism. I vote for Republicans because they believe the way of life my great-uncle died for is worth preserving.

I have no love for Barack Hussein Obama, but if you ask me, things started going downhill when Clinton got elected. President George Bush Sr. was a war hero, just like my great-uncle. He fought for his country. He went to church. He played baseball. He was faithful to the same woman his entire life, just

like the Lord commands. Just like the men in my
family have always done.

Is being faithful easy? No. Commitment is
never easy. Honor is never easy. But commitment and
honor matter. These snowflakes think a video of
locker room talk is the worst thing a politician has
ever done. They didn't have to explain to their
daughter what a stain on a blue dress was made of.
They didn't have to talk about fifty-year-old men and
twenty-year-old girls. Barry Hussein Obama knew
how to keep it in his pants. That is the one thing you
can say for him. Literally, the one and only thing. He
still hated America. He still hated the little guy who
didn't go to Harvard Law. My brother and two of my
cousins lost their homes in '08, and all Barry could do
was give blank checks to big banks.

But there would be no Barry Hussein Obama
without Bill and Hillary. That much I know for sure.
Truth be told, when I woke up the day after the
election in 1992, I realized Satan had gotten his foot
in the door of my country. I knew it wouldn't be long
before everything fell apart.

Kevin

I thought we were operating under some sort
of unspoken truce: I wouldn't place a Clinton sign in
my yard, so long as Rick didn't place a Trump sign in

his yard. Yes, I put the "Love is Love" sign in our yard, but Rick was welcome to put up a sign that read:

IN OUR HOUSE WE BELIEVE
PUBLIC SCHOOLS ARE A WASTE OF MONEY
WOMEN BELONG IN THE KITCHEN
BLACKS WERE BETTER OFF ON THE
PLANTATION
SCIENCE IS WITCHCRAFT

He could have, but he didn't. Instead, he put up a "Make America Great Again" sign, which is a shorter version of the same message. No need for all those words, when everyone knows what you mean anyway. One of those blue signs tells anyone all you need to know about them. Rather than having to walk up to someone and say, "Hey, I hate brown people, think book learnin' is for commies and queers, and oh-by-the-way why do you let your wife wear shoes?" you can just say, "Make America Great Again." When someone throws a #MAGA on the end of a tweet, you know exactly what they believe. You know exactly who they hate.

I don't know if Rick thought of our lack of presidential yard signs as a truce, but I'm pretty sure he knew that once the MAGA sign came out, the gloves were off.

Rick

I stood at the window, watching as Kevin drove every one of those signs into the ground. First was County Recorder, whatever that does. Then state legislators and City Councilman from outside of our district. Finally, five Hillary signs. Five. And behind all the new signs sat his original "Free love is free love" sign.

All of his signs pointed straight toward my house.

"Katie, do you see this?" I asked.

"What is he doing?"

"From the looks of it, losing his mind."

For once Kate took my concerns about Kevin seriously. She didn't accuse me of being a pervert about Marina. Probably because Marina wasn't around. It was just Kevin, driving stake after stake into the ground, his hair finally becoming a little bit messy. He didn't look like Kevin the Rich Guy Consultant. He looked crazy. I have no idea how I lived across from someone that long and never knew he was a maniac.

"I think he saw us," Kate said, looking nervous.

Not knowing what to do, I raised my hand and waved through the window. Just like I always did. He looked right at me and went to the back of his truck, grabbing a sixth Hillary sign. He locked eyes with me and never looked away as he drove his final Hillary sign into his lawn.

"This has to stop," Kate said.

"Yes," I said. Not because I meant it, but because yes is a good word to get in the habit of saying to your wife.

But would I let Kevin win? Heck no. My great-uncle didn't turn tail and run when they fired on Omaha Beach.

And neither will I.

Chapter Eight

Kevin

I became a consultant the same way a lot of people become a consultant: I quit a job I hated and had to figure out how to make money. Thankfully my education gave me the ability to sell little pieces of my time to the highest bidder. The problem with that is there is never enough money and never enough time, especially with three kids to feed, and especially with Becky heading off to college soon. Which means I work a lot of the time and think about work all the time. Literally, all the time. Sometimes my son will catch me staring off in the distance, and he'll call me on it.

"Dad," he'll say, "you're doing it again."

"Doing what?" I'll ask, but I already know what he's talking about.

Of course, things could be worse than just thinking about work all the time. For much of my childhood a steady paycheck and my parents didn't cross paths often. A tent wasn't the worst thing we ever lived in. There was an old farm house we got through my dad's job at a dairy farm that was so bat- and mouse-infested that me, my brother, my mom, and my dad all slept in one room. And there were countless HUD-subsidized apartments.

It wasn't just where we lived. My dad drove a series of rusty, barely running old trucks and my mom's Blazer had one hundred and fifty thousand miles on it when she bought it. My mom had to constantly borrow money from her own piece-of-shit dad, despite working two jobs. Even after his broken back healed, my dad's dyslexia kept him from achieving his potential, and his love of marijuana meant jobs with drug-tests were out of the question.

And there was always the fear.

More than anything else, fear is what I remember about growing up. Fear of the power being turned off. Fear that the government would cut your parents off, even when they were working hard to find a job. Fear that the welfare people would visit and find out your dad still lived at home, that your parents' separation was just a fiction, a fiction you had to perpetuate to your school and your friends to keep the welfare people away. Fear that you would grow up and become like all the adults you knew, bitter and angry and hateful. Fear that you would live the same life of fear your parents lived.

Working all the time to generate a consulting income is incredibly hard. It takes every bit of my time. Even if I wanted to mow the lawn, I would have to choose between the lawn and a game of basketball with Kevin Jr. or a movie with Eliza and Becky. Or a date with Marina. Earning a living this way is not easy.

But is it the worst thing? No. No, it isn't.

Rick

I didn't always sell toilet paper for a living.

For a long time, I put my education to use as a reporter for my community's daily paper. It was all suburb stuff: high school football games, city council meetings, business openings. I wasn't just a reporter, either. I was the photographer for my own articles, snapping pictures of Friday night games and ribbon cuttings. My town is a place where you can raise a family and make a living, and I think I did a good job telling that story. Mostly because it's a true story. The job wasn't glamorous, but the Lord was willing. With Katie's teaching job we made it work, and I was eventually promoted to assistant editor. Like reporter, assistant editor sounds a lot more glamorous than it was. It still meant writing articles and taking my own photographs.

It still meant trading in one used car for another.

It might not have been glamorous, but the job made me feel important. Everyone knew my name. They knew my name because even though my daughters wore clothes handed down from each other and handed down from other kids at church, I had a superpower.

I could make you a little bit famous.

I could give you something you could cut out and mail to your grandmother. I could give you something you would frame behind the counter in your business. I could make the world see you and validate you, at least for a moment. I could give you something that would let the girl or guy who dumped you back in middle school know they had made a mistake.

At the paper, I mattered. Because I could make the world see you, the world saw me. But as an assistant editor, I saw the writing on the wall. Week after week, the conversation became less and less about stories and less about the community and more and more about declining ad revenue. After twenty-three years I was laid off. Jack, the editor, took over my duties. Five months later the paper shut its doors.

Jack manages a call center now.

I tried not to take it personally. I realized I was the victim of circumstances beyond my control. I tried not to blame anyone, but I know the death of the local newspaper is exactly what the Left would want. The Left can't control local newspapers. George Soros can't control the local media the way he can control the national media. Hillary's lackeys were never going to call me and "suggest" that I look more into some bullpucky story about Russians. I wrote real stories about real people, not the garbage on CNN. I was never Fake News. I had integrity.

And then I was gone. Me, Jack, everyone who made their living at the paper. We were all gone.

But the Lord is so good. It wasn't long before I found work as an office supply salesman. I sold the things interns used to order for me back when I worked at the paper, but it was still a steady paycheck. Finding a job in the city as a middle-aged journalist in 2012 just wasn't going to happen. Sales didn't use my degree, but it kept a roof over our heads. It was hard to adjust, though. Really hard.

As a reporter and then editor, I was in demand. Our Mayor, the owner of every McDonald's in town, rich people, powerful people—at the paper they all took my call. Sales was different. A lot different. I never had an off moment. I was under constant pressure from management to push my clients to place their orders online. I wasn't going to do that. I had lost my job to software once. I wasn't going to let that happen again. The pressure wasn't the worst part, though. The worst part was knowing how unimportant I was. Selling printers and paperclips showed me how quickly the public forgets. Two and a half decades as a newspaperman disappeared immediately.

I'll be the first to say that I didn't handle it well. I would talk to clients about my time at the paper and how we were destroyed by the Left and their buddies in Silicon Valley. I talked about Barry Hussein Obama a lot and how he hated America.

Then I made a mistake. I had a customer who owned a little bar and grill where a lot of bikers stopped to get a burger and a beer. The owner of the bar didn't buy a lot of office supplies, so I only saw him once before I made the joke that cost me my job.

"Why should we bury Obama six feet deep?" I asked Charlie, the owner, while he signed the invoice for his order.

"I don't know," Charlie answered.

"Because six feet down all niggers are good people."

It was just a joke. The first time I met Charlie, he was complaining about high taxes and the cost of doing business. I knew he hated Obama. You could tell by looking at him. His arms were covered in tattoos and he drove a truck. A big truck with fake testicles hanging from the trailer hitch. I thought I knew who I was dealing with.

I didn't know Charlie's wife was black. I didn't even mean it. It was just a joke. I was just trying to connect with a customer. Had I known his wife was black, I would have never made the joke, but should I have lost my job over it? Trump is right. Political correctness is destroying this country. What followed were the darkest days of my life. I just…well, Katie put it best.

"Honey," she said, "you lost your mojo. Come back to me."

I never told her what I said. It was the only time in our marriage where I didn't tell her everything. I just said I lost my job because a client didn't like a corny joke I told. She never asked me what the joke was, because I don't think she wanted to know.

Honestly, the specifics of the weeks and months that followed are mostly lost to me. I don't remember spending time with my girls. The only thing I remember about those months was Katie telling me I had lost my mojo, and that I couldn't get an erection for her, at all. I thought it was the medication, so I stopped taking my pills.

This time stopping the pills didn't work.

Truth be told, the only way I could get my willy hard was to form my left hand into the shape of a pistol, put it in my mouth, and use my right hand to masturbate. When I ejaculated it was like I was twenty-two all over again. This is dirty talk, but I dropped loads that I hadn't seen in decades. It wasn't just the thought of shooting myself. I would picture my body hanging from a lamppost or a basement beam and my crotch would start getting warm. It was like my willy was telling me my life as a useful member of society had ended.

One night I walked out to the garage, put the barrel of my rifle against the roof of my mouth, and sat there, trying to think of a reason not to pull the trigger. It wasn't a fear that suicide was a sin. If the Lord wanted me to shoot myself, I would. If he didn't, I wouldn't. You can't thwart the Lord's will.

What saved me was the thought of the Fall Harvest party.

My kids and grandkids couldn't tell ghost stories and eat peanut butter eyeballs in a house where their father and grandfather was found with a hole in the top of his head and his hand on his crotch. You can make a crappy horror movie out of that, but you can't turn it into a party. I put the gun down, and I prayed. I cried, and I asked for the Lord's help.

Two days later my cousin Dave asked if I would like to give janitorial sales a try. I asked what made him think of me, and Dave told me he thought I was a good man.

A good man.

When you've spent weeks ejaculating to the thought of killing yourself after losing your second job in a row, the words "good man" aren't something you're expecting to hear. If you ask most people, I'm just a washed-up old racist.

If you ask Dave, I'm a good man.

I met Dave at a diner near our house to fill out the employment paperwork. I couldn't even make it home before I had to pull over. I was crying so hard I couldn't see, and my mustache was all snotty and gross. I couldn't let Katie and the girls see me that way.

Selling toilet plungers wasn't what I thought I would be doing, not at this stage of my life. I miss telling stories. I miss not feeling like I let the Lord down. I miss feeling important. I miss belonging. I miss going to the bar and never having to buy my own beer, and not because I'm a cheapskate. You know you matter when someone else picks up the tab and buys you a beer.

But the job is better than sitting in a garage with my hand in my pants and a gun in my mouth.

Marina

For our first date, Kevin picked me up at the end of my shift and took me to Denny's. I had the Grand Slam, and he had the Moons Over My Hammy. We were twenty-two, and I asked him what he wanted to be when we grew up.

"President," he said.

"President of what?" I asked.

"President of everything. The President."

"Seriously? What do you really want to be when you grow up?"

"President," he said. "What do you want to be?"

"A stay-at-home-mom. I want to raise Becky and have more kids," I said.

That night I thought Kevin's answer was crazy. Who says they want to be President? Right out in the open like that? Community college students who grew up like Kevin did not become President. Looking back, though, my answer was crazier. What I was saying—and what I know he understood—was that I wanted him to be Becky's dad. I wanted him to raise my little girl. I wanted to have more of his babies. I wanted to build a life with this kid who carried *Tortilla Flats* in his back pocket and wore a puka shell necklace.

It was 2004. Puka shell necklaces were still sexy. At least they were to me.

Kevin didn't run away, the way most guys would have if a single mother had told them on their first date that she wanted to be a stay-at-home mom. But Kevin more than stayed. A few months later we got married and started building our family from literally nothing. We lived in a crappy apartment, and he was only halfway through his bachelor's degree. He worked his ass off to make my dream come true. For years, I was a stay-at-home mom with one of our kids always by my side. Always.

I was there for every big moment in their little lives.

Kevin made that happen for me, for Becky, for Kevin Jr., and Eliza.

For a lot of those years, we were broke. It wasn't always Beemers and new trucks for the Harrisons. We owned three salvage title Hyundai Accents before Kevin's career took off. One of our many Hyundais was so broke-down I used to have to lean forward when we were driving up a hill. I learned how to make almost anything you can imagine using tofu, and not because we're fancy liberals who like tofu, but because tofu is cheap and meat is expensive.

We ate so much tofu that Becky decided she had had enough. She wasn't going to "eat any more toe food." Our daughter was done with toe food. Kevin was done with toe food. I was done with toe food. Unfortunately, we weren't done being poor, so the next time I just put extra soy sauce in the tofu, to make it taste a little less like toe food.

Sometimes I get jealous of career girls like Kate. It would be nice to have something to say when other women started talking about their jobs that didn't make everyone pause for a second. Seriously, if you're the stay-at-home-mom in a group of working women, your response to "What do you do?" will cause the entire conversation to take a beat while everyone figures out what to say that won't offend you.

It's kind of like someone bringing up Trump's wall, and everyone turning to stare at the only slightly Mexican girl in the group.

Plus, I wouldn't mind being validated by someone I wasn't related to, someone who would tell me that I'm doing a good job just because I'm doing a good job, and not out of fear that I'll cut them off from sex or those tiny microwavable pizza rolls the kids love.

Actually, I should say and/or. Sex and/or pizza rolls.

Kevin loves his pizza rolls, too. You haven't been married until you've seen and then tried to unsee a naked man eating pizza rolls.

Those eleven years of being a stay-at-home mom were mostly magical, and then they ended when

Eliza started first grade. Suddenly I was alone, in a new neighborhood in the middle of the country where I didn't know anyone. I tried to push away the thought that my usefulness to society had ended in my early thirties. I became even more jealous of someone like Kate, someone who has purpose and goals when her alarm goes off every morning.

That's why I bought my dog, JK. She is named after JK Rowling. Yes, I love *Harry Potter*. I used to read *The Sorcerer's Stone* to Becky every night, before we met Kevin, when all we had was each other, a library card, and an apartment that was somehow even worse than the one Kevin and I moved to.

Loving *The Sorcerer's Stone* isn't why I named my dog JK.

JK Rowling was a fighter. She was a single mom on welfare, and I'm sure she wouldn't give a shit what anyone thought about her spending twelve hundred dollars on a dog.

Because she had earned it.

I figured out how to feed my babies when all we could afford was dollar menu burritos and toe food, and I'm not going to feel bad about buying a dog.

Kate

I thank God every day that I have a career I love. It doesn't pay well, and sometimes Rick and I have to spend our own money on classroom supplies. But for me, the bad stuff about teaching is still just one percent of the job. It might sound corny, but I make a difference. Every day I wake up, and the world is better off for what I do. I really believe that, and I really believe God himself gave me the chance to do something I love and am good at.

Not everyone is so lucky.

But doing something I love doesn't mean I haven't missed being with my own babies during the day. I never wanted to be a stay-at-home-mom, but I also never wanted to drop my kids off at daycare. Too often people think if you like one thing, you need to hate the other. If you like working, you must hate the idea of staying home with your kids. If you like staying at home with your kids, you must hate the idea of working. Even worse, if you're a stay-at-home mom, you must hate working moms. Or, if you work, you should hate stay-at-home moms.

What's the word—binary? Teaching second graders, I don't get to use words like binary often. It's true, though. People think the world is black and white. It isn't. It's so much more complicated. The world is all sorts of grey. Your life is all sorts of grey.

I love my job, and I would have loved to never have to drop my babies off at daycare. But my girls seeing me work must have made some difference. Every morning they wake up to the sound of me getting ready to go to a job that I love, a job that puts food on their plates and a roof over their heads. Our oldest daughter followed in my footsteps. Anna is a teacher, and she just won her District Teacher of the Year award. I have both of those plaques hanging behind my desk in my classroom, and I can tell you which one means the most to me.

Rick and me, we have a hard life. We have a beautiful life.

Life can be both.

Life can be binary.

Chapter Nine

Kevin and the Monster

I know how to make a monster.

First, start with a man who never had to earn anything in his life. Ever. The man was born with money. The man was born with a family name. The man was born knowing he would never, ever have to wonder where his next meal would come from. The man would go to a good college because that's just what people in his family do. Right after graduation, the man's family would give him enough money to get a head start on a good life.

This man, this future monster, had a good life handed to him. Because of what he was given, as time passes the man gets confused. He believes he worked for the things that were handed to him. The man comes to believe what he was given rightfully belongs to him and is only further evidence of his virtue.

In his confusion, the man starts to become the monster.

The monster starts to believe he can take whatever he wants. The monster believes if it is there for the grabbing, he can grab it. The monster takes what doesn't belong to him. The monster takes what was never his to take. The monster believes he's earned the right.

No one holds the monster accountable for being a monster.

No one ever punishes the monster for what he's done.

In fact, powerful friends try to hide the things the monster has done.

Whether it's women, money, or power, the monster believes he has a right to anything he wants.

That night we had to watch confetti rain down on a monster, and it killed me to see the monster get what he wanted. I have a specific way I hold Marina and the kids when they are hurt. I wrap my arms around them, pull them toward me, and make sure my arm rests against their head in a way that presses my flexed bicep against their cheek. It's my way of telling them there is someone bigger and stronger who can shield them from a hard world full of monsters.

When I was twelve, I started doing pushups behind the fifth-wheel trailer we lived in. I wanted to be strong. I wanted to learn how to protect myself and my family. Life has sharp edges, and even monsters hesitate to fuck with you if they see your shirt stretched tight against your shoulders. Muscle matters. Strength matters. Or, it usually matters.

The night Trump won, my muscles didn't make a damn bit of difference.

My dad believed that violence had its place, that there were problems only a closed fist and a big bicep could solve. He taught me to always hit back. Hitting back takes big muscles, but on election night I was reminded that there are problems a closed fist or a big bicep won't solve. It's a lesson I sometimes forget.

When my muscles didn't help, I tried using my words. I said whatever I could think of.

"He's going to lose the popular vote."

"It will be fine, babe; there is still the electoral college. They don't have to elect him."

"This whole wall thing was all an act. He's just going to want to make more money and cash out."

"He'll get bored and leave after two years, just like Palin did in Alaska."

"We still have President Obama for three more months."

"How much does the President really affect your life?"

"We'll make a Facebook group for people like us."

On and on I went, but nothing I said made any difference.

Marina—the only Mexican in our neighborhood—just watched Trump become President by demonizing people like her. It was too much. She broke down. There was nothing I could say to fix what the Monster broke. That's what I'll always remember about the night Trump won: Three scared children, one sobbing wife, and a husband and dad who couldn't get any sleep because he failed to protect the people he cared about from a real-life monster.

Rick and President Trump

Lord willing, miracles can still happen.

Lord willing, people like us might be able to make a better go of it.

Lord willing, I might not spend the rest of my life selling toilet paper.

Lord willing, with President Trump, my country still has a chance.

It made me glad to see the little man win one. That's what I remember about election night.

Marina and Donald Trump

I guess I took it seriously for the first time that night. Before election day, I let Kevin read all the polls and watch all the news. It's not that I don't care about politics. It's that I have more important things to do than click on every one of the one hundred CNN alerts that pop up on my phone all day, every day. Kevin told me America had become just too diverse and tolerant to elect someone like Donald Trump. He would tell me, over and over, that our country was better than Donald Trump. There was nothing to worry about.

"Maybe twenty years ago, or even just before Obama, someone saying those things about Mexicans and Muslims could get elected," Kevin would say, before launching into some monologue about how many twenty-two-year-olds were likely to vote in some county in Ohio I had never heard of.

"People like us don't have to worry, we are the future," he would tell me. "We just have to wait for all the angry old white people to die."

People like us? I guess he means this version of our family he's created in his head. In this version we aren't Kevin and Marina and Becky and Kevin Jr. and Eliza. We are not a family of people with names and individual opinions and hopes and fears. In this version of our family, we aren't the Harrisons. Being just the Harrisons isn't enough. In this version, we are a white-collar, upwardly mobile mixed-race couple. We send our kids to college and drink craft beer and do whatever else it is that people like that are supposed to do.

Don't get me wrong: Donald Trump being President scares me. It makes me feel like everything I was taught as a little girl was a lie. It makes me feel like all the lessons I learned in my grandfather's hardware store about hard work and the American Dream were wrong. I was glad my grandfather wasn't here to see Trump's people chanting about the wall. When CNN projected Donald Trump would win, it felt like I was in a movie, and not a happy movie. It made me feel like there was something darker in the world, in all of us, just waiting to come up.

That was one reason I cried that night.

The other reason was that I knew this election and what it did to my husband wouldn't be over. For eighteen months all Kevin could talk and think about was the campaign. In his mind, this election and Donald Trump said something about Kevin, how he grew up, and what happened to his mom. No matter where a conversation began, the end was always the same: Donald Trump. Kevin always loved politics, but this election was personal in a way no other election was. For Kevin, this election was about way more than just politics.

My husband couldn't see that this election wasn't personal. It had nothing to do with him.

One night, when I couldn't take any more talk of Donald Trump, I said that to him.

"Kev, you know this election isn't about you, right?"

"It is, babe. It is about me."

There was a pause.

"It's about you," he said. "It's about the kids. It's about all of us."

On election night I cried for America and for people like me who suddenly found out that even in 2016, hate and racism are still a way to win an election. But mostly I cried for me, not people like me. Kevin thinks everything is a fight. He thinks every part of life is a battle he has to train for and win. Donald Trump being President would be no different. After the election, I knew presidential politics wouldn't leave our house for at least four more years, if we were lucky. In Kevin's mind, it would be this new version of our family against the jackass who hosted *The Apprentice.*

It would be war, at least in my husband's heart. It would be a war he could never win.

I used to love hearing Kevin explain things I didn't know about. I'm not like him. I don't read books about problems I can't fix. I am too busy raising three children to think about saving the world, but Kevin is different. I remember him spending our first road trip telling me all about an article he read about a loan program in India.

"Marina," he said, his blue eyes shining, "if you give a woman seventy-five dollars at the right time in her life, you can change everything for her."

He followed that by rattling off a bunch of statistics showing how changing one parent's life can alter their kid's destiny.

"Who knows?" He asked me. "If you change one kid's life, maybe you can change the world."

I didn't know a lot about his family then, but I know now he wasn't just talking about Indian women. If Kevin could change some desperate woman's life, it would be like getting in a time machine and changing his mom's life. That was the Kevin I fell in love with. He was big-hearted and believed he could make a difference, even when I met him and he had forty community college credits to his name and slept on a pile of clothes in the corner bedroom of a HUD-subsidized apartment he shared with his brother.

Finally, after listening to Kevin talk about changing lives and making things better for poor Indian women and their children, I asked him to pull over. We exited onto a little dirt frontage road that ran parallel to the freeway. He climbed on top of me, and we had sex in full view of passing cars. We were just two kids getting down in a salvage title Hyundai Accent, which wasn't that bad considering the alternatives were having sex on a pile of dirty clothes with his brother just outside the door or trying to sneak around in my parents' house—something Jesus would not approve of.

Kevin was close to finishing when he looked up and saw a cop in our rearview window. He pulled out and came all over my belly.

"Officer," he said to the cop at my window, "this is my wife."

I wasn't his wife yet.

But when I looked at what was on my belly, I knew one day I would be. I knew Kevin would raise Becky. I knew we would make more kids, and they would all grow up smart and compassionate and big-hearted. Just like their dad. I haven't lost that feeling, but every time Kevin talks about Donald Trump I feel like I lose a little piece of the man my husband used to be. I assumed that would end on November 9, 2016.

Watching the confetti pour down on Donald Trump, I realized this wasn't the end. That was the main reason I cried so hard that night. And the next morning.

Kate and the President

Rick wanted to be in the military, just like his great-uncle the war hero. He wanted to save his country. He wanted to save the world. Finding out his illness would keep him from becoming a soldier was the biggest letdown of his life, at least until he lost his job at the paper. He bounced back, though. When he was young, Rick could bounce back from bad news better than anyone I ever met. When he found out we were pregnant, he did the strong, silent thing, but after a little while he was there for me. Back then he was my rock. It didn't matter if he couldn't accomplish a specific dream. He would dust himself off and start working on new dreams.

"Poco a poco," he would say, using one of the few phrases he remembered from what little Spanish he picked up in high school. I remembered a fair amount of Spanish from college, but poco a poco is pretty much the extent of Rick's Spanish. Even with all his talk about the wall and illegals, he still loves that saying.

Poco a poco.

Little by little.

Little by little, we would make it work.

God blessed me with a baby too soon, but God also blessed me with a husband strong enough to withstand whatever life threw at us. Rick was strong. He was resilient. He could face whatever our lives had in store for us.

For a while, anyway.

I know my husband has thought about killing himself. I know he's come close to going through with it, at least once. One morning I went out to grab some duct tape from the garage and saw his rifle on his workbench. Rick is never, ever careless with our guns, but it was more than just a rifle left lying around. It was the look in his eyes. There was nothing there. I knew he was lost, but even worse, he knew he was lost.

I would ask him about it.

"Honey, how's your mojo?"

It would be a full thirty seconds before he realized I had asked him a question.

"Oh, I'm fine."

Not a number, like we usually do.

Just, "Oh, I'm fine," with an empty look in his eyes.

By God's grace, his cousin Dave gave him a job selling janitorial supplies, which seemed to help. He started taking his medication again and stopped staring at some far-off place only he could see. The money he makes selling toilet paper is even worse than the office supply sales job, which was worse than the newspaper. Over the last few years our family budget has steadily shrunk, right as everyone in our house started eating like grownups.

I know how hard that must be on Rick. He was once poorly paid but important. Now he is barely paid, and in his mind, at least professionally, not important at all.

But we make it work, and I haven't seen any guns lying around lately.

Poco a poco, I guess. Maybe that's all you can ask for. Poco a poco.

It wasn't just the job that put the sparkle back in Rick's eye. It wasn't just the job that made him look like the Old Rick. The Old Rick came back to me because of Donald Trump. Rick always had more time for politics than me, but ever since his work troubles started he's watched more news and spent more time on the Internet. Sometimes I go to bed and Rick is still on the couch, listening to someone on his favorite channel yelling about this or that. It's not that I disagree with Rick about politics. It's just that I don't have time to listen to people scream at each other for hours. But, the more Rick watched the news the more he liked Donald Trump, and the more Rick liked Donald Trump the more he seemed like my Old Rick.

Me, I don't particularly like the President. I think the new President is a lecherous pervert who needs a haircut. I would never leave the man alone with our daughters. I can only imagine what might happen.

Truthfully though, anyone is better than Hillary Clinton. I am exactly the type of woman Hillary has never respected. Remember when she said she wasn't a "stand by your man" woman, or something like that, in that fake southern accent of hers? Hillary can be whatever she wants, but I am a "stand by my man" woman. When Rick lost his job because of a joke, I stood by my man. When I found a rifle lying on a workbench in our garage, I stood by my man. Even when I see him spying on our neighbor, I stand by my man. And I don't stand by my man because I'm weak or because God told me to. And I don't stand by my man because I depend on him to support us. I make more money teaching second graders than Rick ever has at any of his jobs, as hard as that is to believe.

I stand by my man because I made a commitment to stand by the family we created.

Commitment is important to people like us. Maybe when Hillary went to some fancy-schmancy law school she forgot that, but I don't forget it. Ever. RickandKate are committed to building this family. With God at our side we will see that commitment through to the end.

I will stand by my man, and that doesn't make me a weak person or less of a woman, no matter what Hillary Clinton thinks.

I would never vote for Hillary. No way. Anybody but her.

But, I don't love our new President like Rick does. To tell the truth, I've taught school with President Bush Sr., Bill Clinton, President Bush Jr., and Barack Obama in the White House. It didn't matter who was in charge. There were always new rules and less funding and more of my and Rick's money buying boxes of Kleenex and crayons and pencils. As a teacher I've learned all presidents make promises they don't keep. It's just what they do. No matter who was elected, that wasn't going to change. It's foolish to think any president is a wish-granting genie.

Politics are important. But they aren't the only way to change the world. I've learned when it comes to making the future better, groundings and kisses are the secret. Hard lessons and soft landings do more to change the world than any president ever will.

Rick is different, though. Rick sees something in the new President that he long ago stopped seeing in himself. I think he sees a willingness to fight. He sees a willingness to hit back. Rick once had a little fight in him, and I don't know if it was the layoffs, the medication, or just time, but he lost his mojo. He lost his fight. He found the mojo he thought he lost in our President. Even though the constant Trump talk does drive me a little nuts, it's worth it to see Rick get some fight back in him. If the election had gone another way, I'm not sure what Rick would have done. I needed my husband to get his mojo back. I'm glad he won. He needed a win. We needed a win. Rick, I mean.

I'm glad Rick won.

Chapter Ten

Kevin

Was the blog I posted the morning after the election an exact reflection of what I believed? No, not really. I don't think what's happening in our country will be fixed by more love, or the inevitable bending arc of justice President Obama always talks about. I think conflict is usually only solved one way, especially political conflict. But I felt like the world needed to know where the Harrisons stood. My post was a blog version of our tolerance sign.

By noon it had more than four hundred thousand views.

I felt famous. I felt like I had a voice. I felt like I was making a difference. It was a good feeling. Now I know why writing for the paper was such a big deal for Rick, even if he never made any money doing it. When people care what you have to say, it's an addictive feeling.

After CNN called the election for Trump, I couldn't sleep. Trump wasn't the only monster who won. Rick won, too. He had the last word. For now, anyway. Before I blocked him, I would read his crazy Facebook posts guaranteeing Trump would win. I would read how there were so many more deplorables than the elitist media could ever imagine. I thought he was crazy. I mean, he is crazy. But he was also right, at least about the deplorables part.

Election night 2016 was a good night for men with a family name. Election night 2016 was a good night for monsters. Election night 2016 was a horrible night for my sleep. So, I wrote a blog and posted it on LinkedIn. I made my voice heard. I mattered. And I loved it.

The Morning After
By Kevin Harrison

Now that this election is over, what should we tell our kids? It's a question that populated my Facebook feed late last night and was brought up by more than one pundit as the election reached its (very unexpected) conclusion. And I get it. I felt it. My wife and I have three kids. Explaining how the world works to a child is especially difficult, particularly in moments when you're struggling to understand it yourself.

But ultimately, even though adulthood is just as confusing as childhood, our kids will look to us for understanding, and depending on how your family felt about the election, an explanation. My kids will ask my wife and me what happened, and how this man, of all people, became President.

We will begin that conversation by telling them that creating the country we want to see doesn't begin in the White House.

It never has. It begins in our house. It begins in our living room, not the Oval Office.

We will tell them that an election doesn't dictate whether your home is a tolerant one—a home that welcomes people of different faiths, of different races, of different ethnicities, of different beliefs, of different sexual orientations. We will tell them that an election doesn't dictate whether your home is one that values education and knowledge—a home that encourages all the people who enter it to become educated, and to use that education to help fulfill their potential.

We will tell them that in our house healthcare is a human right, black lives matter, women's rights are human rights, no human is illegal, science is real, and love is love. No matter who the president is.

We will tell them that an election doesn't dictate whether your home is a compassionate home, a home that can serve as a home for anyone who feels scared, broken, persecuted, forgotten, or hurt. We will tell them that despair and terror are no way to live life, and that living in a state of terror and despair does nothing but create paralysis. We will tell them in this moment, in every moment, paralysis is the opposite of what the world needs.

We will tell them our country needs engagement. Our country needs action. We need everyone—no matter what color they are or where they came from—to remain actively involved in creating the types of communities, and the type of country, we can all be proud to live in. We will tell them that their grandparents endured long migrations from Mexico and Sweden, experienced the Great Depression, World War II, the Cold War, the 1960s, Watergate, and much more.

None of it easy, and each of those events came at a steep cost. But it was never the end.

And through it all, we slowly became a better, more tolerant society, even when it didn't feel like progress was being made. We will tell them that in a democracy, sometimes you lose but losing doesn't mean you stop playing. It means you get stronger and you get smarter. Losing means you start training for the next round.

Losing means you stay engaged.

We will tell them that the definition of what it means to be a decent human being was never set by the President. Not by this President, certainly not by our next President, not by any politician. We will tell them that being a decent human being still means what it has always meant: being honest, having integrity, working hard, and standing up for those who can't stand up for themselves.

We will tell them that the world hasn't ended.

We will tell them that in America we don't elect Kings and Queens.

We will tell them about their mother's grandfather, who came to America an immigrant and died a business owner and former mayor.

We will tell them that the same country that gave us George Wallace also gave us Martin Luther King Jr., we will tell them that the same country that gave us Frederick Douglas also gave us Jim Crow, and we will tell them that in America nothing is easy, nothing is final, and that everything is earned the hard way. To quote Dr. King, "The arc of the moral universe is long, but it bends toward justice."

We will tell them that there is work yet to do, and that when it comes to creating a better world, there is always work yet to do, and that that work never ends with an election. And we will tell them that their mom and dad love them, and that everything is going to be okay.

Rick

"Did you see this?" Kate asked, handing me her phone. It was an email from her vice principal. He had forwarded her Kevin's blog, probably assuming she was just as liberal as every other member of the teacher's union.

"What? Kevin is a political expert now?"

"Did you see the views?"

I had. You couldn't miss the view counter at the top of the blog. Three hundred thousand views, last time I checked. Kevin wrote a blog that was read by a decent-sized city.

The privileged jerk had taken this from me, too. It wasn't enough to come to my neighborhood and constantly rub his money and his new cars in my face. He had to take my old job, too. Or at least a version of it. If Trump had won four years ago I might have written the editorial for my paper's opinion page. Not anymore. The only person on my street writing about one of the best days in our country's history is my idiot liberal neighbor. And he's making it sound like election night was the apocalypse.

> Four years ago, people would have been emailing my editorial around. Now, I get to read Kevin's

blog.

"I saw that. Crazy."

Crazy that my neighbor can't see how good election night was for America. Crazy that my neighbor has the time to write for free, when I'm working my butt off selling toilet paper to scrape up every penny I can. Crazy that the best morning I've had in a long time is ruined by the arrogant know-it-all who lives across the street. Crazy that what I used to do for a living my neighbor now does as a hobby. Crazy that even when I think I'm getting ahead I'm reminded that I'll always be less than a guy with an expensive haircut and a Beemer. Crazy that it seems like every time I take a step forward the world knocks me back.

Crazy that overeducated privileged liberals like Kevin keep ruining my mornings and getting me fired. Yes, it's a crazy world. Crazy. Crazy. Crazy.

"Marina sent me an email," Kate said.

"What?"

"Earth to Rick? Earth to Rick? Marina sent me an email."

"Oh."

Probably forwarding her husband's blog post.

Ha! We already read it, Marina. And it was pretty shitty the first time.

Marina

When I got done with my morning cry, I found Kevin staring at the computer, watching the blog he wrote in the middle of the night go viral. I was proud of him. I hoped writing would help, if he kept it up. If he felt like he was making a difference, maybe he could let go of a little bit of the anger inside of him.

I sat down on his lap and watched the view count increase by ten thousand or more every time he hit the refresh button.

"I'm so proud of you," I said, kissing him on the cheek.

"I know, right?"

He hadn't heard a word I said.

"I emailed Kate. We invited her and Rick over for dinner."

That got his attention.

Kate

The basement is mostly Rick's part of the house. Because of that, it's a mess. Except for the one corner he keeps clean. In that corner there is a desk and an old computer that doesn't work anymore. On the walls are framed copies of his favorite articles from his time at the paper. I used to think he kept the basement corner clean because one day he would write something. Maybe he would try freelancing for the paper in the city, or even write a book about his great-uncle. I hoped he would do something that would make him feel like he mattered again.

I let go of that hope a long time ago.

For me, Rick's job at the paper seems like a different lifetime, but I don't know what it's like to lose something you love. I still have the family I love. I still have the man I love. I still have a job I love. I still have the life I love. It's a hard life, but I haven't had to experience the loss of anything truly important to me. Rick has. Now that loss is sort of like his illness. It's not something we can cure. It's only something we can manage. We manage it by not arguing with him when he blames Obama for our little hometown paper closing.

We manage it by quarantining twenty years of his life behind a door we never open.

Normally when me or the girls say something that reminds him of the paper, he lashes out. Not in a violent way. My Rick is not a violent man. His voice will just get an edge to it. It's an edge that lets me and the girls know we're treading on rocky ground, and that if we say anything else we're likely to hear a twenty-minute tirade about George Soros and Barack Hussein Obama and Hillary Clinton.

During dinner.

This morning was different. I honestly didn't connect Kevin's blog with Rick's time at the paper. Kevin's post on LinkedIn was just a silly little thing. It was another way for our neighbors to get attention. It was another way for them to tell the world they are better than the rest of us. Just like their BMW. Just like Kevin's haircuts. Just like their yard sign.

Silly little things.

Silly little things that don't add up to a whole lot. A sign doesn't make a difference. A Facebook fight doesn't make a difference. You know what makes a difference? Writing stories about good people in your own community. Teaching poor kids from the ghetto how to read. Buying Kleenex for your classroom out of your own pocket. Selling toilet paper at a job you hate so your daughters can eat. Those things matter. Those things make a difference.

Silly little things like blog posts don't change the world. They don't even change your street. They are just more noise.

Rick obviously didn't see it that way. He didn't snap, though. His voice didn't get an edge to it. I didn't hear anything about Obama or Soros or Syrian refugees.

That morning he just…faded away.

Rick was there, and then he wasn't.

Chapter Eleven

Marina

"You cannot be serious," Kevin said, pushing me off his lap and shutting down the computer.

Apparently, the idea of having Rick over for dinner was enough to distract him from being internet famous.

"I am. I am absolutely serious. Kate emailed me back, and we're having them over for dinner on Friday," I said.

Kevin would be glad to keep this stupid feud up for the next hundred years, if that's what it took to win. I was happy to let it go. Did I agree with Rick and Kate about politics? No. But there is more to life than politics, and having a feud with the couple across the street wouldn't un-elect Donald Trump.

"We are having them over, and you're going to be nice, and we are not going to talk politics," I said.

"Uggghhh. Politics schmolitics," Eliza said from the kitchen counter.

Our kids have varying levels of interest in politics, usually in direct proportion to how much time they spend with Kevin. Our son, Kevin Jr., is our most woke kid. Ha! Look, I try and stay cool.

Woke. That's a word now, and our son is definitely woke. Kevin and Kevin Jr. can ride their bikes all day and talk about who will be the next president and why. Kevin Jr. is different than his dad, though. He's thoughtful and considerate, always making sure doors are locked and lights are turned off and car keys can be found. That's not really Kevin Sr.'s thing. He can walk into a client's office and instantly come up with a solution to their problems. But left on his own, every light in the house would be on and the side yard gate would be wide open.

Eliza, our youngest, is like a concentrated version of Kevin. She's a warrior through and through. Everything is a fight—except she could absolutely care less about politics. Eliza bounced back first on election night with a simple statement on the Trump era:

"I'll make my own way," she said.

I believe she will. Maybe not at eight years old, but one day.

Becky was interested in politics when she was little. Then she became a teenager and got a job and started planting the seeds of her future life as an adult. Her biggest concern is how to pry her boyfriend away from some new war video game every boy on the planet is playing to pay attention to her.

Whenever this particular issue comes up, Kevin always weighs in with, "I don't get it. In high school I would have crawled through broken glass just to get a chance at some boobs."

I don't love the way Kevin voices his confusion with the boys in Becky's class, but I agree with his point. I don't get boys today, either. Ignoring something good that's practically trying to throw itself in your lap for some pointless war game is just crazy.

"Rick and Kate are coming over for dinner. You're going to be a decent person. We aren't going to talk politics. This battle with Rick? It ends now."

"Mar—"

"Stop, Kevin. I'm serious. It's done. It's over. We are moving on. Period."

I had spent the last year and a half hearing about Donald Trump and Hillary Clinton and blue-collar voters in Ohio and Pennsylvania, states I have never even been to. Oh, and a wall separating Mexico and America, and what that wall meant for people like me. I was done with it. If I never heard the words Clinton and Trump again, it would make me the happiest woman on the planet.

"And," I said, "we're going to re-friend Rick and Kate on Facebook."

We have a life to live. We have children to raise. I have parent-teacher conferences and reading time and making sure Becky doesn't finally find a boy who can manage to pull himself away from video games long enough to get her pregnant at eighteen, just like her mom.

Ain't nobody got time for no stupid Facebook fight.

There I go again. Look how woke I am.

Kate

Marina is beautiful. I'm pretty sure she wakes up with makeup on, and her clothes are very, very tight. Her clothes are also bright. The woman loves neon. When she isn't sunbathing on her porch she's out there in her tight pants and high heels, smoking a cigarette with her little dog on her hip. If anything is ever out of place on her, I haven't seen it. She even manages to make smoking look classy.

It isn't just her looks. I've been in her kitchen. It isn't like our kitchen. In our kitchen every drawer is pulled out. Empty chip bags blow across the floor like tumbleweeds. Four girls—four smart, amazing girls—and not one of them ever learned how to shut a cupboard. The sink is full of dirty dishes, and there is usually a half-eaten and crusty pot of Kraft Mac n' Cheese on the stove that Rick will slowly pick at for a day before I scrape it out and put the pot in the dishwasher.

Marina's kitchen is spotless. I have never seen a single dish in the sink, and the first time their kids ever ate Kraft was at my house the week after Kevin's mom died. It's all organic food in Marina's kitchen. If it were possible to have organic, fair-trade, gluten-free, grass-fed, free-range Mac N' Cheese, I'm sure Marina would have it.

I know Rick likes her. I know he watches her from the window sometimes. It isn't just her big hair or her tight, neon clothes. It's also the way she's polished and perfect and always offers Rick lemonade when he's mowing the lawn. That's the other thing: who has time to make freshly squeezed lemonade? My kids get lemonade-flavored Kool-Aid.

Though they do squeeze the packets themselves.

I'm not going to be that woman, though. I'm not going to be the woman who can't handle a pretty, polished female who wants to be her friend. Marina has had a different life than me. She married a guy who dreamed bigger dreams than just writing for the local paper. She can afford to stay home and squeeze lemons. She can afford to make sure her skin stays smooth and beautiful. She isn't getting up at 5:00 AM to feed kids and a husband before going to work and earning the biggest paycheck in her family.

I love my life, but my neighbor has had a much easier go of it.

I'm not going to hate her for it.

Marina

It was a lovely dinner, if you ask me.

I made Carne Asada from free-range, grass-fed bison and homemade tortillas. Kate and I had a nice red wine and I made Rick and Kevin shandies using fresh-squeezed lemonade.

I'm pretty sure Rick had never mixed his beer with lemonade before, but he seemed to like it.

Seeing Rick and Kevin sitting opposite of each other was strange, and not just because they hate each other. Kevin and I got married so young that he's become my expectation of what a man should look like. He has a thick chest with nice shoulders and a trim waist. Not a hair is ever out of place on his face or his head. He never leaves our room without a collar on, unless it's to go into the side yard and do his pushups and pullups.

Rick is different. He and Kate are older than we are. Rick is tall and thin, except for his big belly. He wears shorts that end halfway down his thighs. Even to a dinner party. Kevin never, ever wears shorts. Rick's hair is mostly gone, and when he talks he speaks in short half-sentences. Kevin's hair is thick from the anti-balding medication he's preemptively used for years, just to make sure his hair wouldn't leave him like it did his uncles and grandfathers. And with Kevin, everything is a complete sentence. Usually many complete sentences, with no break in between. Everything about Rick feels loose at the edges. Everything about my husband, even his beard, feels tight and controlled.

It's not that Rick is unattractive. I don't think of him that way. It's that he's so different than Kevin, and we don't have many couples over for dinner, especially since Kevin let it be known that the Harrisons are the neighborhood liberals.

During dinner, Kate caught me staring at Rick. Or, staring might be a little strong. She caught me lingering, looking at her husband when he wasn't speaking.

"Everything okay, Marina?" Kate asked me.

"Oh, sorry. Yeah. Sorry. I was just thinking the program I volunteer at might need a new cleaning supplies company. Rick, do you want me to do an introduction?"

"Thank you, Marina, but I'm okay. Too many clients as it is, you know?"

"I get that, buddy," Kevin said. "Believe me, I get that."

One day a week I volunteer at a program for homeless teen mothers. Becky and I were never homeless, but I could imagine a world where we were. It's my way of giving back.

And the offer was my way of being nice to Rick.

Kate

We went home after the pistachio ice cream, after Rick and Kevin agreed to set their differences aside and become Facebook friends again. Marina made them do that, and it was a little weird. It reminded me of making two boys in class shake hands after one of them throws an Elmer's glue bottle at the other. You know they're just shaking hands because the teacher is making them, not because they've actually seen the error of their ways.

Or because they really want to be friends.

"So, what did you think?" I asked after we settled into bed.

"About what?"

"Earth to Rick, Earth to Rick. Dinner."

He was fading away again.

"Oh. Eh. Food was good. Marina did a good job."

"I bet."

That lifted the fog and brought my husband back to Planet Earth.

"You bet? What's that supposed to mean?"

"Rick, don't treat me like I'm stupid. I see the way you look at her. I get it. She's really pretty. If I were you I would stare at her too, just try—*try*—not to make it so obvious. Especially when she's staring back at you."

"Stop it, Kate. I do not stare at her."

He took a pause, then asked the question I knew he really wanted to ask.

"Was she really looking at me?"

"Oh my gosh Rick, are you serious? She was looking at you the whole time. The whole time."

Once in a while, sometimes against your better judgement, you have to give your husband something to keep the bounce in his step. There is nothing more dangerous in a marriage than a husband or wife who doesn't feel attractive and has to go looking for it somewhere else.

"Of course, she was looking at you. Kevin's a pretty boy. I think she liked seeing a real man in the house," I said, patting his belly. It's the spot he knows I like. It's the spot I can push against and rub on until I finish in bed.

"Baby," he said, "You know you're my girl. Plus, my willy would never work for a woman who paid twelve hundred dollars for a dog."

"Rick, don't say those things!...is that really what their dog cost?"

"Yep. She told me how much their dog costs. Right in the kitchen. Like it was something to be proud of."

"Come over here," I said, pulling my husband's body toward mine.

The lights were off. Rick was big and ready. It was so dark, but I hope his eyes were wide open.

Kevin

Rick obviously hates Mexicans. He couldn't take his eyes off Marina the entire night. I know what he's thinking. He doesn't even have to say it. I could see it on his face.

He's thinking, "How does an illegal afford a twelve-hundred-dollar dog?"

He's thinking, "We've got to get that wall built, right now."

At least we get to be Facebook friends again. I have that to look forward to. I get to see all his #MAGA crap all the time. I get to see more memes about locking Hillary Clinton up. Facebook friends with Rick again. Great. #SMITH.

Stands for #ShootMeInTheHead.

Rick

What type of man buys his wife a twelve-hundred-dollar dog?

The type of man who doesn't mow his own lawn. The type of man who has all of his college degrees on the wall in his dining room, hanging right above his wife's head. I read them during dinner: Magna Summa Cumma Duma Rumma Laude with Distinction and a big gold crown, or whatever. Like he's the first person in the history of the world to get a college degree.

A college degree is not that impressive. I have one, and I sell toilet paper for a living.

And a twelve-hundred-dollar dog? Three of those dogs are worth more than our car. Even if I could find Marina physically attractive, any woman that tells you how much her dog costs is instantly unattractive. Instantly. Like my brothers and I used to say, a woman like that is a total boner killer.

Chapter Twelve

Kevin

Immigration Does Not Destroy Working Class Jobs
by Kevin Harrison
Guest Contributor
The Globe & Tribune

If you ask my neighbor, immigrants are to blame for the two jobs he's lost in the past five years. But most economists believe the benefits of immigration far outweigh the costs.

And my neighbor? I can tell you immigrants had nothing to do with his job losses. But what happens to a local economy when a large number of low-skilled immigrants find their way to one spot in America all at once?

In 1980, with the Cuban economy suffering Fidel Castro told Cubans if they wanted to leave, they could go—and he would even find boats for them. Castro might have had a patchy beard and a well-developed appreciation for violence, but in this instance, he was a man of his word. In what became known as the "Mariel Boatlift," more than one hundred thousand Cuban refugees landed in Florida between April and October of 1980.

Many people, as you can guess, didn't welcome the new arrivals with open arms. One of the primary concerns was that low-skilled immigrants would depress wages and employment for Miami's working-class residents.

A decade after the refugees arrived, one economist decided to see what impact the Mariel Boatlift had on the Miami economy. In his study, "The Impact of the Mariel Boatlift on the Miami Labor Market," Berkeley economist David Card concluded that despite a seven percent increase in the Miami labor market for unskilled workers, the mass migration had virtually no impact on local wages and unemployment.

In other words, the immigrants who landed in Florida were absorbed by the economy. More people means more workers, but it also means more demand for the products those workers consume. Cuban refugees needed jobs, but they also needed to eat, buy t-shirts, wear shoes, shave, wash their hair, and do all the other daily tasks that require human beings to purchase something from the store. The demand created by these new consumers creates additional jobs.

Of course, some Cuban immigrants became more than just low-skilled laborers. Immigrants and the children of immigrants have a disproportionately higher rate of starting businesses—so it goes without saying that several businesses in south Florida got their start when a large group of people started boarding boats at the Mariel Harbor in Cuba.

When it comes to the economy, people talk about pies, and how they get divided. However, the idea that the amount of pie is finite—and the arrival of new Americans means less pie for the rest of us— is just incorrect. New entrants into the economy inevitably mean more pies. But maybe you're not a pie person. Maybe you want something new and different—and immigrants expose us to the new and different. Sometimes new Americans arrive and do the big things we often cite as one of the main benefits of immigration, like starting Fortune 500 companies. More often, refugees and immigrants are absorbed into existing communities. My wife's grandfather immigrated to the United States at the tail end of the Mexican Revolution. He would later settle in a small town, start a hardware store, get elected Mayor, and most important, start the family that would eventually give me my wife.

America's economic strength is that we are not finite. If you don't believe me, ask economist David Card. In fact, ask any economist.

Just don't ask my neighbor.

Rick

One viral blog, and the paper from the city asks Kevin to write an op-ed.

The same paper that had no need for me or anyone else who used to make their living writing about small-town suburban life. And of course, the op-ed is on immigration. He can't get over the fact that his wife is Mexican. It's like some sort of badge of pride he wears. Like it takes some sort of special skill to be born in Mexico.

Kevin deciding he's going to take my old career from me isn't even the worst part. The worst part is that he calls me out in the first paragraph. Kate tried to calm me down. I showed her the headline, and the byline, and she said, "Honey, this isn't about you."

"Kate, this is literally about me. Read it."

She read it and handed it back to me.

"This is a silly little thing. This is Kevin pretending to be an expert. He just wants the attention. You know how he is. Let it go."

"Let it go? Let it go? I'll let it go when he stops calling me out in the bullshit he writes."

"Language, Rick. Language."

"Language? Why don't you talk to Kevin about his language?"

"Because I am not Kevin's wife. Let this go,

Rick. Be the bigger man. We are trying to be friends with them."

Friends? Friends don't take the things that mean the most to you. Friends don't call you out in an op-ed for the entire neighborhood to see. Friends don't steal your voice.

Dear Kevin,

I would appreciate it if you didn't call me out in these blog posts you've been writing. It's not cool. If you ever want a lesson in how to be a real writer, let me know. I did that once. I was good at it. I would be glad to give you the help you need.

Sincerely,

The Monster Across the Street

PS I would tell you to f*** off, but I don't normally use that sort of language. Plus, our wives are making us be friends. Don't do anything like this again. Ever. I mean it. Don't you ever call me out like that. I mean it. EVER. Asshole.

Copy. Paste. Send. See, Kate? We can be friends.

Chapter Thirteen

Kevin

Al Gore was the reason I went to college.

I know that's a weird thing to say.

Bush/Gore was the first presidential election I ever voted in, and I remember staying up late that night watching the CNN coverage. The next morning, I went to work, wanting to talk politics with my coworkers, when I had two realizations:

No one wants to hear a nineteen-year-old's opinion on presidential politics. And, if I didn't get my shit together, no one would ever want to hear my opinion on anything.

The first realization came courtesy of my coworkers. The second realization was all mine, and without it, I wouldn't have my degrees. I wouldn't have my career. I wouldn't have Marina and Becky and Kevin Jr. and Eliza. I wouldn't have a blog that got read by more than five-hundred-thousand people. I wouldn't be writing op-eds for the newspaper, like I was Woodward and Bernstein.

The day after Bush/Gore, I went home to the HUD-subsidized apartment I shared with my brother and wrote "$50" on a calendar stuck to our fridge. Fifty dollars was all the money I could set aside from my next paycheck for my new college fund. A year and a half later I took my meager savings and enrolled in community college.

Forty credits later I met Marina and Becky. Two months after we met, I called my mom to tell her I was getting married, and after an extended silence she asked, "Well, what does she look like?"

"I don't know? Dark?"

That was my answer. In my defense, my family is all blue-eyes and blonde hair. Marina is the darkest person in my family. I had no problem describing Marina to male friends from back home who hadn't met her, but this was my mom. I couldn't exactly go into Marina's physical attributes. The best I could do was the unfortunate, stupid description of "I don't know? Dark?", which led to my mom's follow-up question:

"How dark is she?"

The tone of her voice clearly communicated that dark was not the preferred shade for her daughter-in-law. My mom's idea of beauty was Princess Diana, not the short, curvy, Salma Hayek-looking girl I married.

"Mom! I don't know? I think she's Mexican."

My mom was a Democrat, and tolerant right up to the point when she thought her future grandchildren might be several shades browner than her sons. Then she reverted to her more natural state, which was closer to a 1930s Democrat than a President Obama Democrat. Closer, in other words, to the Trump "Democrats" in bumfuck West Virginia.

I expected her to ask if Marina was actually from Mexico, when the wedding would be, or even if Marina was pregnant. Instead she said, "You'll never finish college."

She was wrong.

I finished in just under four years with one bachelor's and two master's degrees, all while working full-time and helping Marina raise our new family. One semester I had to get a waiver to take thirty credits. That's how hard I worked to get my education. It wasn't handed to me.

My degrees don't come from an Ivy League school, and as a consultant, where you get your degree matters. I get a little embarrassed when an Ivy League colleague comes over and sees I graduated from nowhere state university—but I do have my degrees hanging on the wall. Most people I know stick their diplomas in a closet or lose track of them.

Not me.

Those degrees say important things about me. They say my kids don't know what government cheese tastes like. They say my kids will never buy their winter coats on layaway. They say in our house, terms like bankruptcy and foreclosure are things you hear about on TV, not words whisper-shouted between parents in the hallway. They say that the money and food the government gave my family when we were poor, broke, and living in a tent wasn't a waste. It was an investment.

More than anything though, those degrees say one really important thing about me and the family Marina and I created: In our house we don't ask questions like "How dark is she?"

Rick

My family earned our right to be here. My great-great-grandfather was from Germany and knew how to brew beer, so he got a job at the brewery practically right off the boat. It was hard, sweaty, dirty work, and the pay was awful. Especially if you don't count the twelve beers they gave workers during their shift.

I don't need Kevin or any other smug leftist to tell me about one hundred thousand Cubans coming over and making Florida better, or whatever he said in that op-ed. I know we're a nation of immigrants. I know that. I went to first grade. I remember the Mayflower.

It isn't just the murderers and the rapists and the gang members that make me so angry.

It's the free healthcare. It's the free Hussein Obama cell phones. It's the in-state tuition. It's handout after handout, while people like me and Kate do the right thing and constantly struggle. We have paid a medical bill every month of our entire marriage, right from the start. We are always in hock to some pediatrician or gynecologist. None of my kids had a cell phone before they could buy their own, and every single one of them will have to pay their way through school with jobs or scholarships.

Nothing was ever handed to me and Kate. We had to work for everything we've ever gotten, and even when we qualified for handouts I wouldn't take them. We've earned our little place in the world. If the Mexicans want to come here, fine. But they need to do it the right way. My people did it the right way. They crammed their way into rat-infested ships and went through Ellis Island.

They didn't come here and take anything from anyone.

Truth be told, I don't care if Marina's people come. As long as when they get here they know there are no handouts, and they have to work their asses off. Just like my great-great grandfather did when he got here. Just like I do today. Kevin should know that. He didn't get where he is from taking handouts. He has all those degrees on his wall, and that's earning it too. In a way. Kevin isn't driving a Beemer because of a handout. That's why I don't understand why he's on their side.

That's wrong. Yes, I do. I know exactly why Kevin is on their side. I know exactly why Kevin believes no human is illegal.

He's blinded by a brown woman. He's put a piece of ass on a pedestal.

And it's made him forget who he is.

Chapter Fourteen

Rick and Kevin on Facebook

Rick Sullivan updated his status.
Seriously, these liberals would win a lot more
elections if they didn't call everyone they disagreed
with a Nazi. There are two sides to every story.

Kevin Harrison
Except for actual Nazis, right Rick Sullivan? It's okay
to call an actual Nazi a Nazi.

Rick Sullivan
Who's a Nazi, Kevin Harrison?

Kevin Harrison
The Nazi, Rick Sullivan. The Nazi who killed the
woman. In Charlottesville.

Rick Sullivan
Don't know that yet, nothing has been proven.

Kevin Harrison
Proven? Rick Sullivan, the guy admitted it. He is a
confirmed Nazi.

Rick Sullivan
I didn't see that.

Kevin Harrison
Not seeing it didn't stop you from commenting? You mean, you took the time to give your opinion to the world on Facebook, but didn't even bother to read the latest news before you did it?

Aaron Fries
shit just got real

Rick Sullivan
Kevin Harrison you mean #fakenews? No, I didn't take the time to watch fake news, if that's what you mean.

Mike Turnbull
Kevin Harrison Rick Sullivan the election is over, you two. Didn't you get the memo?

Kevin Harrison
Rick Sullivan you didn't bother to read or research before you commented? Is that how you wrote your articles back in the day? No wonder I'm doing what you used to do.

Rick Sullivan
Kevin Harrison you don't have to get personal. I warned you about this, about calling me out like this.

Marina Harrison
Kevin Harrison Rick Sullivan PLEASE PLEASE
STOP THIS! SERIOUSLY STOP

Rod Butler
Hey Kevin Harrison, keep calm and listen to your
wife.

Kevin Harrison
Rick Sullivan I do get personal when we're talking
about Nazis. It makes me angry. Like most sane
people. What is wrong with you? Doesn't this bother
you? Weren't you taught better than this?

Rick Sullivan
Kevin Harrison Your an arrogant jerk. You know that
right I'll say a prayer for you. I really will.

Chad Polley
I'm just here to read the comments.

Rod Butler
I'm just here to watch Michael Jackson eat popcorn.

Kevin Harrison
Well, better an arrogant jerk than a racist Nazi. Maybe
if you weren't such a racist prick you would have kept
your last job. We're friends with Charlie's wife. She
told us what you said. Say a prayer for yourself.

Marina Harrison
Kevin Harrison Rick Sullivan STOP ENOUGH

Rick Sullivan

Kevin Harrison You seriously want to do this? You seriously have time to fight with me on Facebook like a little girl? Why don't you go out and mow your lawn before your gardener screws that wife of yours. He can tell a whore when he sees one, I guess.

Kevin Harrison

You're going to talk about my wife, Rick Sullivan? Fuck you, you piece of fucking shit. I have a better job than you, more money than you, and people actually care what I have to say. Who the fuck ever cared what you have to say? A shitty little community paper? You're just pissed because it's finally dawned on you that no one gives a fuck about what you have to say. Ever.

Rick Sullivan

Do you know you're not wanted here? Has that not dawned on you yet? That you don't belong, or are you just too stupid to get it? Leave this neighborhood Kevin Harrison no one wants you here white trash

Kevin Harrison

Seriously, seriously. Rick. I'm supposed to feel bad for all you Trump supporting lazy pieces of shit that somehow couldn't or wouldn't realize that the world is changing? You worked at a community paper and it never dawned on you that your days might be fucking numbered? Seriously, how fucking stupid are you? I know you look at my cars. You know how I got those? I worked fucking hard. I got an education. Then I got more. I work twenty hours a fucking day.

What did you do? Used your daddy's name to go to school and then knocked up your ugly fucking high school girlfriend. Lazy? fuck guys like you who do the minimum, always, Rick, and then wonder why the fuck your always behind do you know what I would give to be born into a family that had its name on the fucking street of the town I lived in? And all you could turn that into was a job selling fucking toilet paper and knocking your wife up? And somehow that's President Obama's fault that untalented, lazy, mediocre pieces of shit like you can't make it now? So what, so you go off and call him the N-Word rather than getting off your fat ass and doing something about it? Your problem isn't President Obama or Hillary Clinton. Your boy Donny T became President and didn't get you a better car or a better looking wife. A president isn't a fairy fucking godmother, you piece of shit. Do more than the minimal, motherfucker, and stop expecting someone else to fix your shit for you. Jesus isn't going to save you and neither is Donald trump

Rick Sullivan
Wow. You know, your right Kevin. I was born into a family with a good name no wonder your a liberal, kid like you no wonder your mom swallowed those KILLED HERSELF swallowed all those pills like WHITE TRASH

Kevin Harrison
FUCK YOU MOTHERFUCKER

Rick Sullivan
LIKE I CARE WHAT YOU THINK WHITE
TRASH

Kevin Harrison
I THINK YOU DO CARE WHAT I THINK
MOTHERFUCKER

Rick Sullivan
like me or anyone else cares about the opinion of a
WHITE TRASH elitist rich little faggot like you has
to say??? Please lol WHITE TRASH

Kevin Harrison
White trash????? Says the guy with a fucking Goodwill
couch AND A DODGE FUCKING NEON. I need
to wipe my ass rick, do you have any toilet paper? It's
the only thing you're fucking good for. Seriously, have
you ever thought about killing YOURSELF? I would
if I were you

Rick Sullivan
FUCK YOU FUCKING PUSSY YOUR
WELCOME TO NEVER FUCKING TALK TO
ME AGAIN YOU'RE YOUR WHORE TO GO
BACK TO MEXICO THIS USED TO BE A
DECENT NEIGHBORHOOD UNTIL THE
TRASH MOVED IN FUCK YOU

Kevin Harrison
You need to stay on your side of the fucking street
fucking Nazi peace of shit fucking Jesus freak
COWARD lord willing Rick you can FUCK OFF

Rick Sullivan
SHUT THE FUCKUP ABOUT THE LORD
WHITE TRASH PIECE OF SHIT

Kevin Harrison
I'm serious, you fucking piece of shit You say one
more thing about my wife and family EVER YOUR
DONE MOTHERFUCKER

Chapter Fifteen

Kevin

When I was thirteen my mom found work as a legal secretary, and my dad finally got a good job working the line at a rubber products manufacturer. After years of living in subsidized apartments, a tent, a trailer, and a bat-infested farmhouse, my parents could finally have a real home of their own—though my dad couldn't stomach the idea of living in a city, or even a town with a decent-sized population. Instead of buying a home in the suburbs, a home like the one I live in, he bought land about forty-five minutes outside of town and began building a log cabin.

The "community"—if you could call it a community—that we moved to mostly consisted of trees, moose, and a collection of summer houses owned by wealthy lawyers, financial planners, and insurance brokers who lived in the city.

That, and church camps.

Once a summer my brother and I would ride our bikes down to the start of the dirt road that eventually led to church-owned property, large summer vacation homes, and the small, square cabin my dad built with a bit of help from me and my brother. At the bottom of the road, around the end of July, hundreds of blonde-haired blue-eyed Christian girls would stream into the camps. My brother Cory and I would watch as they emptied out of their buses, filled with optimism that somehow we would lose our virginity to not just one Christian girl, but an entire bus full of Christian girls.

Those church girls may have tolerated our presence, but the wealthy owners of the summer cabins did not. They had their own little homeowners' association, which had never done a lot—until we moved in and disrupted their perfect Promised Land. Once we arrived, a bunch of conservative, small government, Reagan-worshipping corporate attorneys and CPAs started passing rules and ordinances like it was the New Deal.

First, my dad built a log fence around our property to give our dog room to run.

Turns out, the height of the fence was *just* over the height allowed un`der the new ordinances.

"I apologize, Mr. Harrison," they said. "It will have to be torn down."

"Unfortunately, no, it can't just be shortened, because as you can read—if you know, you weren't just ignorant white trash who worked in a dirty rubber factory—Section II, Subsection A clearly states that all fences must be approved by the structural committee and ratified by the Board and Executive Committee *prior* to construction."

"*Prior* to construction."

In case we missed that part.

"We know you, um, we know you probably haven't dealt with an HOA before, but trust us, we're just trying to do what's best for the community. Yes, we know your red metal roof is brand new—but again, if you will note Section Four Subsection C of the Aesthetic Ordinance, you'll see that green is the only permitted color for metal roofs. Blends in with the scenery. It's more natural. Less intrusive."

"Don't you think?"

"When did we pass the ordinance? Oh, I think it was two meetings ago? Meetings are held every second Tuesday of the month. And, just so you know, you'll need a shirt and tie. I can lend you one if you need one. You know how it is. I hate government and someone telling me what to do more than anyone, believe me. President Reagan was right, government is the problem. In a community like ours though, we have to maintain...standards. The community needs to maintain a certain level of quality. For the sake of property values."

"I'm sure you understand," they said.

My dad understood. He understood perfectly and had the most appropriate response one could have: Fuck that. He did not repaint our roof. He did not put a tie on and start attending HOA meetings.

However, he did take the fence down, and in its place purchased trees to strategically plant along the edges of our property. One of the problems we had was summer home people cutting through our lot on their brand-new four-wheelers. The trees would serve as a natural fence, and at their full height offer the added bonus of preventing anyone from seeing our cabin. True protection from an overreaching government run amok. True protection from the elitist assholes on the board of a homeowners' association, in other words.

After planting the trees, we learned that the problem wasn't our original fence, or that we hadn't gone through the proper channels to get approval. The problem was that we were there at all—any other complaint was just a polite way of telling us to get the fuck out, that our type didn't belong. That point was driven home when my dad and I watched Don, the president of the HOA, climb into his brand-new lifted truck, drive down to our property, and use his giant tires to crush the trees my dad purchased, leaving every one of them broken and destroyed.

After Don finished his work my dad, watching what his neighbor was doing from behind our living room window, said, "Kev. Go get in the truck."

My dad had an old, nasty truck we called Gangrene. I went down and got in the passenger seat, and my dad climbed in the cab a few minutes later. From there, the chase was on. We flew over a rutted dirt road, broken wood and sawdust and Coke bottles and empty cans of Natural Ice rolling around the bed of the truck. It didn't take long for Gangrene to catch Don's F-350. When we did, my dad went full-on

Dukes of Hazard and cut him off, blocking his path down the dirt road.

My dad and I got out of Gangrene as Don descended from the cab of his F-350.

"Don," my dad said.

"Bobby! How's it going?"

Grinning, like he didn't just destroy the trees my family could barely afford. Grinning like God had appointed Don the gatekeeper to the better life my parents wanted.

My dad didn't answer his question, and instead kept walking toward Don. We were the only three people in the world, or at least the only three people on that dirt road. The sky was bright blue, the clouds were high and white. What happened that day is one of my clearest childhood memories.

"Bobby? You know those trees weren't approved by the landscaping committee—"

Don was prevented from citing whatever subsection of the landscaping committee's charter prohibited my dad from planting trees on his own property. My dad shoved him, hard. A split-second after the shove my dad put his left hand behind Don's head. As soon as Don's skull made contact with my dad's hand, he grabbed a fistful of Don's silver hair, holding him in place.

The shove was surprising, but not totally unexpected. My dad believed Steve Earle's "Copperhead Road" was his personal New Testament, and my brother and I were raised not to take anyone's shit—and sometimes not taking shit requires more than just a friendly discussion. Sometimes not taking someone's shit requires a little muscle.

I learned that day that not taking someone's shit sometimes requires a little more than just muscle. My dad pulled a large silver handgun from inside of his jacket and jammed the barrel into Don's mouth.

"Don't fucking move."

I also learned that day that your eyes open really wide when you have the barrel of a gun in your mouth. They should. Being that close to the abyss should make you see the world and your place in it with great clarity. Don tried looking at me with those eyes, as if to say, "You're going to do this in front of your kid?"

My dad caught the look.

"Don't EVER look at him again. Look at me. LOOK AT ME!"

At that moment I saw Don wet himself. A large, dark spot began spreading across the front of his pants, slowly. Before that day I thought that just happened in movies.

"LOOK AT ME!"

When Don's eyes were locked on him, my dad said something I'll never forget:

"If you ever come on my property again, ever, I will kill you and your whole family."

He didn't say, "I'll kill you and your whole family." He said "I will." My dad was a conjugator, always spare with his words. The fact that he said "I will" to make his point clear has always stayed with me. He pushed the gun further down Don's throat, making him gag and retch before pulling it out. The whole time Don was gagging my dad used his left hand to hold his head in place, making sure his eyes were locked with Don's, even as thick saliva and tears started to roll down the barrel of my dad's pistol. When Don started crying, my dad knew he had made his point.

We left Don in the road, tears in his eyes and a stain on the front of his pants.

After that day we never heard from the HOA. Apparently, Don realized something about my dad: He meant what he said. My dad always followed through and had Don set foot on our property, I have no doubt my dad would have killed him and his entire family.

Just like he said he would.

My parents would lose our cabin in foreclosure less than four years later, six months after my dad lost his job at the rubber factory to a machine. Apparently if you're a banker you can get away with whatever you want, but if you're a regular guy who loses his job, the bank can take the house you built with your own two hands.

That cabin was the one time my parents ever tried to extend their reach, and all they grasped was devastation. It wasn't all the bank's fault, though.

My dad was a cliché, another middle-aged guy who couldn't see the writing on the wall. Losing that home broke my parents, and what followed was divorce, drug addiction, deep despair, and eventually, for my mom, suicide. Today our cabin is just another summer home, probably owned by some financial planner who inherited his practice from his dad and used his small fortune to buy the home my dad and brother and I built. I drove by when I visited my hometown for my high school reunion. Today the roof is the required green. It is compliant with the ordinances set forth in the Aesthetics Clause. The lot our cabin sits on is entirely free of any fence or tree that would obstruct the path of a fellow rich guy's four-wheeler.

Until that day I didn't know my parents owned a gun. We were rednecks, but I didn't think people like us owned guns. My parents partied when Bill Clinton got elected. Pulling a gun on someone just wasn't something we did. We weren't those people. We were liberals, after all.

Over the years I've told this story so many times Marina has tired of it.

It's understandable.

At first, I told the story to make people understand what I was running from, what I was trying not to be. I didn't want to be the type of person who asks questions like "How dark is she?" or threatens to kill a man and his whole family. For the first years of my adulthood, this story was motivation, one of the cracked, jagged, and angry building blocks from my childhood that I hoped to use to write the story of a better life than the one my parents lived.

Then, when I became a consultant, the story of what happened that day on the mountain became part of my personal brand.

When I meet with clients, I am the liberal with multiple college degrees and a BMW and a pretty wife and three kids who are polished and accomplished in a way that I never was—but I also grew up listening to Steve Earle and Hank Williams, drink Coors, and have cowboy boots in my closet. Oh, and if clients need more proof than that—if a client is a blue-collar Trump guy at heart and needs to be reassured he's not hiring some overeducated snowflake libtard who doesn't know how the real world works—I tell him (always a him) about the time my dad stuffed a gun down our neighbor's mouth and told him that he was going to kill his whole family.

"Fucking HOAs anyway," I can say. "If you want to see government overreach, start with your HOAs."

Drop a line about government overreach in any boardroom in America, and all you will see are nodding heads.

Except none of the repackaging and branding and storytelling ever answered a question I had when I was seventeen, and thought my dad was going to kill a man in front of me.

Why did my dad buy a gun in the first place? Not, why did he pull the gun on Don—given what happened, I understood why he was so angry that day. The bigger mystery was why we owned a weapon that could turn one angry moment into a life sentence. Trees and fences and roofs weren't worth killing people over. Something so small wasn't worth spending the rest of your life talking to your sons through prison plexiglass, your every communication limited, monitored, and sad.

I thought that way when I was a kid, when I was younger, when I hadn't yet earned something of my own. Today I am about the same age my dad was when he stuck a gun in our neighbor's mouth. I get my dad now. It's like that Hank Williams, Jr. lyric, "I think I know what my father meant when he sang about a lost highway."

I think I know what my dad was thinking when he promised our neighbor he would kill him if he trespassed on our property again.

Against long odds, my dad had gone out and gotten a little piece of the American Dream for himself. He built something for his family, my family, and some asshole neighbor who thought we were white trash didn't like that. Some asshole neighbor thought we didn't belong. The fact that my dad was willing to buy a gun tells me just how seriously he took someone trying to take what he had earned. What happened that day wasn't some silly dispute between neighbors. It was about way, way more than just petty bullshit like trees and fences and HOAs.

There was a far more important point to be made. It was a point about belonging, about who deserved to be there and who didn't, about someone who never had to face a struggle—much less choke back tears while their kids were choking down government cheese—trying to take what was yours, or at least make you feel so unwanted that you had no choice but to leave. It wasn't about fences. It was about showing that you'll do whatever it takes to protect what you've earned.

Making a point like that is always worth buying a gun and jamming it down someone's throat.

Kate

It wasn't the rifle in his hands that made me finally realize Rick had stopped taking his medication. It was the visible erection he had as he stood in front of the computer screen, looking at Facebook. His medication had a way of getting in the way of our intimate moments. Even when I wore my prettiest nightie, and I knew he wanted me, it was still usually a struggle, one that often ended in tears.

Rick's tears, usually.

That wasn't the case tonight.

I looked at his pajama bottoms and could see that his willy was no longer our biggest problem.

"I am going to kill this—"

"Stop Rick! What?!? Who are you talking about?"

I genuinely had no idea who or what had made him so angry, so out of control.

"Kevin! Fucking little bitch—"

"Rick! Enough! There are children in this house!"

That was the other thing: Cussing. Rick really wasn't one to cuss. He would usually substitute words that made his cussing corny and endearing. Bullpucky. Fudge. Fudging motherfudger. If he was taking his pills, no matter how angry he got, no one was ever worse than a fudging motherfudger piece of pucky. Yes, he would sometimes use racial words like beaner and junglebunny, but never the really bad ones.

That was the real Rick. Instead, what stood before me was a foulmouthed fully erect stranger with a rifle in his hands.

"Let me see," I said. I needed to see what was on his screen.

"It's okay, I—"

"LET. ME. SEE."

"Hang on, it—"

"Rick," I said, my stomach turning at what I read. When I have to speak before any group larger or more sophisticated than a classroom full of second graders, I get nervous gas. It smells awful. Looking at the screen I could feel something even worse than nervous gas bubbling inside of me. "You called

Marina a whore. She wants to screw the gardener? Who are you? Why are you saying these things?"

"Look what he said about you," Rick said, believing that somehow this was justification for his own actions.

"Rick. I don't care what Kevin Harrison calls me or thinks of me. I would be fine to never think about Kevin again, and just go on living our lives. Why can't you do that?"

"He called you ugly."

"Rick, listen to me carefully. I need you to hear me. I DON'T CARE WHAT OUR NEIGHBORS THINK OF ME. I care what you think of me. I care what the kids think of me. I care what God thinks of me. That's it. Do you read yourself here? Seriously? It's humiliating. Two grown men arguing like teenage girls. Over what? Over what? Tell me? Over what? Politics. Something that happened in Virginia? Guess what, Rick? You need to stop worrying so much about who's in the White House and start worrying about your own house. Seriously."

"What the hell is that supposed to mean?"

"What the HECK is that supposed to mean? Seriously? It means since when did you think it was okay to talk to me like that? Since when did you think it's okay to use profanity where our children can hear? When did you think it was okay to spend your night staring at the neighbor's house or trolling the internet? THERE IS MORE TO LIFE THAN DONALD TRUMP."

"Let me get this straight. I bust my ass at work all day, and all you can do is scream at me because I want to be informed?"

"Informed? That's what you call this? Being informed? Watching four hours of TV every night for the past two years is being 'informed?' No, Rick. I'm not screaming at you for 'being informed.' I'm not screaming at you at all. I'M TELLING YOU YOU'RE LOSING IT AND YOU'RE GOING TO LOSE US IF YOU DON'T COME BACK TO REALITY AND STOP CUSSING AT ME AND PUT THAT GUN DOWN RIGHT NOW!"

"I won't lose shit. You know that."

He finally put the gun down. My foulmouthed, fully-erect stranger of a husband was also apparently arrogant and entitled, but at least he was no longer armed.

"You won't, will you? TRY ME. And when I go, you can't crawl over to Marina, now that you called her a whore on Facebook."

"Crawl over to Marina? What does that mean?"

"Do you think I'm stupid?"

"What?"

"Simple question: DO. YOU. THINK. I'M. STUPID. Do you think I'm stupid, Rick?"

"Of course I don't think you're stupid. Why would you even say that?"

"You don't think I see the way you look at her? You really don't think I know you?"

"I love you! Kate, I love YOU."

"I know you love me, but I know you like looking at her. Just admit it."

"You know why I look at her? Seriously? I don't like Mexicans. There. I said it. I don't like Mexicans. I don't like them coming here, I don't like them taking our jobs, I don't like them living off us. I don't like dialing one for English in my own country. They are thieves and criminals and drug dealers. I look at her and I wish she wasn't in this neighborhood. She doesn't belong here. She doesn't belong on our street. Period."

"So, you're a racist, not a pervert?"

"What can I say. I'm sorry. I am what I am."

"This is my choice. My husband is either a racist or a pervert."

"Sorry."

"Keep your eyes off of her, okay? I believe you, but I won't if you keep looking at her."

"Got it."

"And seriously, Rick? Stop trolling the internet. Stay off of Facebook. Block him again."

"Block him? And let him win? No. Not going to happen."

"Whatever. If you want to act like a child, act like a child. But please, please. Please take me seriously. You need to pray. Right now. Get on your knees and get right with the Lord. This is getting out of control. You need to have the Lord help you get back to who you really are."

I left him there and went into our room, hoping the girls hadn't heard that. But I'm pretty sure they did. When parents fight, kids act like they're trying not to get eaten by the T-Rex in *Jurassic Park*: Don't move and never take your eyes off the monster.

That's the important part.

Never, ever take your eyes off the monster.

Sometime in the night I felt Rick crawl into bed, his familiar belly pushed against my back, his mustache tickling my ear as he whispered "I love you" before falling to sleep.

I don't know if he prayed. I sure hope he did.

Chapter Sixteen

Kevin

Rick wants to bring God into this? He wants to call me an asshole on Facebook and say he's going to pray for me? I learned all I ever needed to know about God when one night, in my early twenties, my dad told me a family secret.

"Kev," he said. "You know, I might die. And your mom might die. If we do I just want you to know that you have a sister."

These are things your dad tells you when he's strung out on meth and can't find any more taco shells in the cupboard or Kraft singles in the fridge. Once he's done eating literally everything in your apartment, he has to find something to occupy his time, so he starts telling you family secrets. At eleven o'clock at night. After you've gotten home from your job and finished your godawful homework on Net Present Value and are so burned out and tired you're sleeping in your clothes, belt and all. Shoes and all, even.

The fact that I had a sister wasn't a huge surprise.

In one family photo book there is a little girl's picture wedged between a picture of me and my younger brother. In another there is a copy of an old Ann Landers column asking for advice on coping with giving a daughter up for adoption. When I was a kid, even when I was old enough to possibly piece together what I was looking at, I just rushed past those pages. They did not align with my understanding of the world, so I kept a wall between me and what the picture of the little girl who kind of looks like me might mean.

Then, high on meth, my dad tore that wall down.

The most important part of this secret wasn't that my mom had a child before me. It wasn't that I had a sister. The most important part of this secret was that my dad isn't the dad of my sister.

My sister was born nine years before me and four years before my parents met. Once my dad told me about her, I wanted to know more about my mystery sibling. So, I called my mom to ask her about the child, and what I got back was irrational screaming, followed by a clear threat:

"This is not your business. If you do not leave this alone you are no longer my son."

Like my dad, my mom was a conjugator. "You are," rather than "you're," meant that she was serious about her threat. Despite her threat, I didn't leave it alone.

Over the years I had conversations with my uncles, my dad, and a few people who knew my mom from that era. I thought back over her life, the drug problems, the struggles, the constant sense that something was deeply off about her relationships with her family of origin. I tried to track down information on my long-lost sister, and my mom followed through and stopped speaking to me. Like my dad, my mom did what she said she would do.

Finally, a private investigator told me what I was already coming to suspect: the father of my mom's baby was her own father. My grandfather.

Growing up I knew my grandfather well. He kept boxes and boxes of pornography that he knew my brother and I looked at and sometimes stole. He had a full head of highly sprayed blond hair and a Chevrolet Blazer that was never more than two years old. He was always marrying someone new, and between 1978 and 2000 he had seven wives, each one younger than the last—and each with a blonde-haired, blue-eyed teenage daughter. Despite being an adult with children of her own, my mom always had a fondness for my grandfather's stepdaughters, treating each like a little sister she needed to watch over.

Treating each of them like someone she needed to protect.

Despite everything she endured, my mom didn't cut my grandfather out of her life. Like a lot of trauma victims, she still desperately needed his approval, and was still convinced that someday something would change and he would become the dad she needed—not the monster that broke her.

But someday, like the song says, never comes.

Before all that though, before the shiny new Blazers and the dyed hair and the every-two-year rediscovery of the gym, subsequent weight loss, and brand-new wife, my grandfather was a deacon in his church. My mom grew up a on a farm in the country out west. It was on the farm, when she was just a child, that her father began to sexually abuse her. That abuse culminated in a pregnancy when she was just fifteen.

The bishop at my grandfather's church made sure no police investigation followed. There was a family name to protect and prominent local church and business leaders would be humiliated. My mom was shuffled off to a program for unwed pregnant teenagers that helped facilitate adoptions of the babies born to girls in the program. My grandfather was protected by the relatively wealthy and powerful people who lived in his little slice of rural America. He was a monster, a monster people made excuses for.

A monster others protected.

A monster who got away with it.

A monster who believed he was entitled to anything he wanted.

A monster who was never held accountable.

My grandfather never stood at a podium while confetti rained down on his head, but he lives a pretty good life. I hear he has a new wife, and a new Blazer. As far as I know, he's never been tempted to swallow a whole bottle of pain pills just so he can stop thinking about what happened in 1972.

My mom never saw her baby, never met her little girl. For a while she received pictures of her daughter, a healthy, smiling little baby who looked just like my mom. Just like her, and a little like me. One of those pictures ended up in the family photobook, wedged between photos of me and my brother Cory. I found the rest hidden away in an old jewelry box while cleaning her house after she committed suicide. Born just fifteen years apart, my mom and her daughter could have been sisters, the same big smile, the same shiny sunshine-colored hair. Instead they were strangers, never meeting.

When I think of God, I don't think of Rick Sullivan. I think of my mom. Where was God in 1972? Where was He? Seriously?

WHERE THE FUCK WAS GOD IN 1972?

When my grandfather was walking my mom out to the barn at the back of their property, was He in the Oval Office with Billy Graham and H.R. Haldeman trying to answer Richard Nixon's prayer that Watergate just go away? Is that why He couldn't hear my mom's sobs? When my grandfather was in my mom's room, warning her to keep quiet or my grandmother would hear, was God busy answering Roger Staubach's prayers that the Dallas Cowboys win the Super Bowl? When my mom was in her hospital bed, crying over a tiny baby girl she would never touch, whose beautiful baby scent she would never breathe, was God too busy tossing some interracial couple into the fiery pits of hell to answer my mom's prayers that she and her baby girl find a way out, a friendly and safe ride as they hitchhiked their way toward a better life and a better world, one where the people you love and trust don't lock doors and tell you that if anyone ever finds out, they'll kill you, and if they don't kill you, they'll make sure your brothers and your mother know what a filthy whore you are?

WHERE THE FUCK WAS GOD IN 1972?

I can tell you where He wasn't. He wasn't anywhere near my mom. He wasn't anywhere near a hay loft in an abandoned barn on the edge of a farm in the middle of nowhere. He wasn't in a teenage girl's room that was decorated with posters of the Monkees and pictures she drew in junior high art class. He wasn't anywhere near my family, trying to protect people I love from a monster. Apparently in 1972 there were just more important things to do than to try and stop some monster of a man from grabbing something that wasn't his, that never belonged to him, that he had no right to grab.

What I do know is that for my mom, the loss of her daughter was just too much to take. Knowing what I know now, I don't think she ever got over the loss of her first baby. I believe whatever light was in her died the moment her little girl was taken from her. The mom my brother and I were raised by was running on fumes. Her years with us were lit by the weak afterglow of a light my grandfather extinguished in 1972. In the forty-two years between the birth of my sister and my mom's suicide she was able to keep a straw out of her nose and the pills out of her mouth for twenty of them, or the exact number of years it took for my brother and me to make it to eighteen years old.

God might be real. I have no idea. No matter what Rick thinks of me, I am humble enough to know that a marketing consultant doesn't know all the secrets of the universe, no matter how many degrees are hanging on his wall.

For all I know, Rick might be praying to the same God who ignored my mom in 1972. He might be praying that God will help him win this fight or argument or feud or whatever it is that's happening between us. Praying that somehow, he'll come up with just the right Facebook post that will make Marina and me want to leave this neighborhood. Or maybe praying that we'll just leave, and his street can go back to being the Mexican and liberal-free utopia it once was.

Rick can keep praying. Rick can pray all he wants. It doesn't matter to me, because I know that if God is there, He's not listening to Rick.

He's not listening to any of us.

Rick

During all my years as a reporter, I almost never covered a crime. At least not a serious crime. It just doesn't happen here. We have vandalism. We have the occasional car that gets broken into. A fight down near the bars. But nothing really serious. In the city? All the time. A couple of years ago I read a story on the internet about a guy who was just walking along the street when three black kids beat him to death with golf clubs. Golf clubs. For no other reason than pure boredom.

Boredom.

That's what this world is coming to. Rather than going out and learning to be the next Tiger Woods, these kids were so bored they used their golf clubs to beat a guy to death.

I got called out to a crime scene a grand total of one time. Once. That was all. It was a meth lab, back when meth was the drug of choice. Back before heroin came into the public schools. The lab was in an old farmhouse in the country, out where the highway runs parallel to the river. The County Sheriff called and asked if I wanted to come and take pictures and write up a story. This wasn't normal protocol. The deputy on scene thought a story in the local paper would be a deterrent. He thought it would make kids think twice about where their meth was getting made and whether they wanted to put those chemicals in their bodies.

The lab itself was a nondescript broken-down old home with faded white siding. The lot was overgrown and there was garbage in the yard—but nothing that made me say, "Hey! I bet that's a meth lab" when I drove by.

It was different when I went inside.

The scary part wasn't the dirty beakers and tubes and all the stuff that really did look like it was stolen from a high school lab, just like that TV show about the drug-dealing science teacher. That crap is exactly what you expect in a meth lab. The chemicals weren't scary either. They have to make meth out of something, and there's more to it than rat poison and cold pills.

This is the only way I can describe the scariest part: When you walk into a room you never really notice the carpet or the color of the walls. They are just an accepted part of the reality you're in. That sounds a little fancy, but that's the best way I can describe it. The floor of the lab was strewn with broken glass. There were dried bits of blood everywhere. The floor was literally covered in bloody glass. The mix of broken beer bottles and beakers shone in the setting sunlight coming through the kitchen windows.

Like wallpaper, sharp edges and blood were just an accepted part of this particular reality. I suppose most makers of meth are also consumers of meth and don't always have a steady hand, which led to a lot of broken beakers. Even worse, the detective told me they likely walked around barefoot. That's where all the blood came from. The drug shuts off their ability to feel pain like normal, healthy people.

"No surprise there," the detective said. "I was at a conference and one of the speakers told me this story of a guy who got bit by a rattlesnake in the middle of a weeklong run on this stuff. Didn't even notice the bite until he sobered up and saw his leg was three times its normal size and totally hairless."

"Totally hairless," he said once more, shaking his head.

It wasn't just broken glass. Knives and razors and needles and all sorts of sharp things were everywhere. They were on countertops and under couch cushions. Worst of all, they were on the floor. Razors with blood on them would stick to the bottom of your shoe. That lab smelled like blood and sweat and feces and every sort of smell that could come from a human body. Layered over that smell was an awful, unnatural chemical scent.

I get queasy at the sight of blood. Truth be told, I get queasy at the sight of anything that might even make me think of blood. I just lose it. I can barely stand to shave. Between that and the chemical smell, it was too much. I raised my hand to an officer, ran outside, and threw up violently off the side of the porch. The breakfast Katie made me was all over my chin, and I had a really bad taste in my mouth. I didn't have any water with me, so I went around the back of the house to see if the sprinkler faucet would work. I couldn't imagine going back inside, much less drinking from any sink in that place.

There, in the back of the house, at the edge of the yard, was a dirty little boy in a diaper. The officers didn't even know a little boy lived in this hellish place, or at least they hadn't mentioned the child. He was out on his own, with no idea where to go or what to do.

"Son? What's your name?"

He didn't answer. He just looked at me. I don't know if he was scared. I don't know if he didn't know his own name. I yelled for the officers. A female deputy came over and picked him up. I saw the bottoms of his feet. They were absolutely shredded. You couldn't tell where the blood ended and the dirt began. With so many open cuts, I was surprised a massive infection hadn't killed the kid or at least cost him his feet.

"I'm going to call my church," I said, before I knew I was going to say it.

I'm sure there is a procedure the Sheriff's office follows in the event a child is found at a crime scene. I'm almost just as sure the normal procedure doesn't involve calling a church. Cops are people too, though. They were busy choking back tears. Both for the little boy and for the fact that had I not had such a weak stomach, we might have missed him. He was just a few feet from a trail that led straight down to the river.

The pastor did what pastors do and went to work. He got the basic facts about the boy, then called the church's social service office. The boy was eventually placed in a foster program and adopted by his foster family shortly after. For a couple of years, I would get updates on the boy through my pastor. His name was Trevor. Against long odds he was relatively healthy. With the right love and a good family, this boy could make up for his tragic beginnings and actually make something of himself.

I really hope he did. I'm going to believe he did, and I don't mean I'll choose to believe like I just ignorantly assume things always turn out okay. I know they don't. Sometimes things go horribly wrong. But Lord willing, this boy whose parents were so messed up will have a happy life. Or, at least a happier life than the one he would have had if the Lord didn't put me in his backyard.

When Kate said the Lord told her we would have a little girl, I knew she was telling me the truth. I knew it. I didn't have to hear from the Lord himself to believe Kate. The Lord worked through Kate to get to me. I will forever love Him for it.

But that day at the meth lab, the Lord worked through me directly.

My belief didn't get even stronger that day because my pastor helped the child. If given even a few more minutes, the deputy likely would have remembered protocol, and the boy would have been placed into some sort of program. He was a cute little white kid. He would have been snatched up and adopted no matter what agency or organization took the lead. Truth be told, if we weren't so broke, I might have adopted him myself. Lord willing, one more baby in the house would have been fine. Katie and I have survived worse.

I would love to have a son, a strong little boy who would carry on the family name.

My belief in the Lord grew even stronger because that was the first and only time I was ever called out to a crime scene. I was there for a reason. Had I not puked and gone looking for a way to rinse my mouth out and clean myself up, there was a good chance that the kid would have been found at the bottom of the river. If he was found at all. It's not like there were pictures of him on the mantel or drawings stuck to the fridge with magnets. There was no evidence a child lived there. The kid was wearing the only diaper in the entire house.

That's how the Lord works. That's what liberals like Kevin—the liberals who ask "If God is so powerful why does he let bad things happen?"—don't get. The Lord isn't a magician. He can't just up and pluck Trevor or some kid from the city out of a bad situation like He was some sort of wizard. Trevor might grow up to be fine. Or the circumstances of his life might break him. Even the breaking has a purpose. A broken person can also be part of the Lord's plan.

The Lord has a plan. He uses us to move that plan forward. I know Katie thinks I'm breaking. I know she's worried about me. I know she thinks I'm losing it. She's told me that I've said and done things over the past few weeks that I would never do. Things I would never say. Things I would never even think. That's why she's asked me to pray. And I will pray. I mean, I am praying. The Lord had a plan for me the day I found Trevor. He put me there at that farmhouse for a reason. Sometimes, when I think about what I wanted Kate to do when she was pregnant with our first baby, or the way I felt after thinking about killing myself, I remember that day with Trevor.

The Lord has a plan for me. I know it. He's good, our Lord. My Lord.

He didn't abandon our country. He didn't abandon my President. And he won't abandon me.

Marina

I grew up in a very Christian, very dysfunctional family. Except, my family isn't like Kevin's family. On the surface we don't look dysfunctional. On the surface we look totally normal. No one in my family ever pulled a gun on anyone. We didn't listen to Hank Williams. My parents had money. Some of it they earned, but most of it they inherited when my mom sold my grandpa's hardware store. But just because your family inherits money doesn't mean you'll have an easy life.

I try to tell Kevin that, especially when he makes unfunny jokes about me being an elitist.

My parents are attractive people. My dad, even at age sixty-three, is still running marathons. He is immaculately groomed. I never saw him with stubble. There was either a beard or no beard, none of that in-between scratchy, patchy growth. My mom is incredibly beautiful, even in her early sixties. I saw the way Kevin looked at her the first time he came over to my house, and I knew what he was thinking: This one won't go south after forty. I'm not saying the way my mom looked in a summer dress is the reason Kevin married me three months after he met me, but I'm not saying it isn't.

Growing up, I wasn't beautiful. Or at least I didn't think I was beautiful. I was short and thick. My boobs and butt got attention, but that's not the same thing as being told you're pretty. This was the '90s, way before being thick was sexy. It was way, way before people would say things like "You're thicker than a bowl of oatmeal" and know it would be taken as a compliment.

Our littlest daughter, Eliza, tells me that all the time, and I love it.

Kevin is right; the world is worse off because of the Kardashians, and they are probably one of the reasons we have this idiot in the White House. But that family did a lot for brown girls with big butts. Thank you, Kim. You made the world safer for people like me.

It wasn't always like that. To my parents I was the fat daughter they were forced to take to church, an embarrassment to a family who valued looking pretty on Sunday above all else. I heard about my weight all the time. First with subtle suggestions about going to the gym, then not-so-subtle suggestions about dieting. Then one Sunday my mom looked me up and down and came right out with it.

"Honey," she said. "You're fat."

How do you get a fat girl to lose weight? I have no idea. I do know how you get a fat girl to eat more, take up cigarette smoking, and start wearing clothes that are even tighter on her growing body.

You tell her she's fat. When you can bear to look at her, you look at her like her very presence is a betrayal. Then you ask Pastor Frank to tell her how she's defying the Lord by using her tight clothes to torment all the boys in church. For extra effect, make sure the pastor's eyes never leave her breasts the whole time he's telling her what a godforsaken harlot she is.

If you're a dad and want to make sure she starts sleeping with the first older guy who tells her she's pretty, you not only tell her she's fat, you consciously avoid her body at all costs. No hugs, no kisses, no sitting next to each other on the couch, no holding hands. No more trips alone together. All of that has to stop right when she gets her first period. You're probably weirded out by your little girl having the same things on her chest you look at in porn, and struggle to deal with that.

She won't know that, though. She'll have no idea. She'll just think she's fat and gross and that's why you make sure there is at least one whole couch cushion between the two of you.

No matter what.

So, how do you make the girl lose weight, get a sexy haircut, and start putting effort into her looks? First, you send her fleeing into the arms of a shithead. Then she gets pregnant. When she finds out she's pregnant and tells the shithead, the shithead picks up a coffee cup and throws it hard, right at her belly. The shithead didn't want a baby. The shithead says all eighteen years of this girl is trying to sink her teeth into his meager "fortune" and take it all for herself. All the rusted bikes, broken down trucks, and shit the shithead inherited from his mother—the girl found a way to break a condom just so she could get half of all this.

Half of what the shithead thinks he earned.

Maybe the weight loss starts when the shithead leaves the girl and her daughter (who back then was his daughter, too) by the side of the road, eight miles from home, and she walks. In the summer. Out west, where the dry heat is still more than a hundred degrees. Maybe she starts to shed a few pounds then.

But the real weight loss starts when she can't take any more thrown coffee cups, or any more jokes told right in front of her about how she's nothing more than a gold digger. In private, the shithead doesn't even try to dress up what he means and just calls her a whore. So, one day she's done. She leaves. She moves into a shitty little apartment with her little girl.

She keeps getting thinner. Stress helps a little bit, but what really does the trick is eating one meal a day. She doesn't do this to starve herself. She doesn't do this because she's going back on the market and wants to look her best. She does this because she can't afford to feed herself more than that and still feed her daughter.

And suddenly, she's thin. She's wanted.

Men start calling her a MILF and do that guy thing where they don't hear her tell them she has a little girl because they're too busy looking at her boobs, and she knows she should hate it and expect more of them but it's nice when someone buys her dinner. She always orders something really big and takes half, usually more than half, home to her little girl. If guys say anything at all about the huge platter she just ordered it's usually something about "loving a girl who eats," but she knows they say that because they want to fuck her, and not because any man she's ever known loves a girl who eats. She doesn't fuck them, but her little girl gets to taste lobster ravioli and Korean short ribs and food that is supposed to be better than anything the little girl can possibly eat, but still somehow tastes worse than a dollar menu bean burrito coated in Cheeto dust.

Eventually she has nowhere to go, so she goes back to the home of the family who believes getting closer to God means wearing fake eyelashes on Sunday. Her father tells her she's welcome to come home, on one condition: She must go to church.

Pastor Frank is very happy to see her again.

Then she meets a guy who can't afford to buy her dinner. He's a community college student and lives in a crappy little apartment, but he carries a copy of a book she likes and tells her he wants to be President. He isn't perfect, not by a longshot. But he tells her she's beautiful, all the time. And he means it. His favorite parts of her are the stretch marks he thinks she got from the little girl he will one day adopt but are really from the weight she carried when she was fifteen and her dad made sure she knew he thought she was fat. She falls in love fast. She can see how broken and angry he is, how he hates the God who sat between her and her dad on the couch, the God that looks over Pastor Frank's shoulder as his eyes linger on her breasts. At first the kid's anger is sexy and powerful and makes life exciting.

Then, as the years pass, the man's rage and constant need to prove himself makes her sad.

She wishes he could finally let the anger go, because she loves him so much, and she's never wanted anything more than this life they worked so hard to get and try so hard to keep.

Kate

"Belief, that's the most important part of a marriage."

I told our oldest daughter that the night before her wedding. It's the same thing I've told every young woman I know who's gotten married. Many of those women were once students in my class. Belief is more important than anything else in a marriage, even love. Belief in a God who has brought the two of you together. Belief in yourself. Belief that you have what it takes to be a good mom and a good wife and still have something left for yourself. Belief in your husband, and that even when he's off-track, God will be there to show him a righteous path.

Sometimes the righteous path God uses to guide your husband is Haldol or Xanax, but that's how God works. It's like that parable: A man is stranded on top of a house in a flood. He prays for God's help to save him. A boat arrives, and the man tells the boat driver, "Hey, God is coming. I prayed. Go rescue someone who actually needs your help. God will save me." After that, a helicopter arrives, hovers over the man, and drops a ladder. The man refuses, again telling the pilot to spend his time saving someone who really needs it.

"God is on his way," the man says again.

Finally, the Coast Guard comes along and sends a rescue swimmer. What does the man do? Same thing.

"Move along, Mr. Coast Guard man. I have God on my side."

Then the man drowns.

In Heaven the man asks, "God, why didn't you save me? I prayed to you. Did you not love me? Why did you abandon me?"

And God says "Listen, dummy, I sent a boat and a helicopter and the Coast Guard, and you kept saying no! How did you think I would save you?"

That's Valium and Klonopin and Abilify and every other medication and combination of medications Rick has tried taking to deal with being bi-polar. Pharmaceuticals are the boat, the helicopter, and the swimmer. We pray for Rick to get well and manage his illness, and God sends Rick's psychiatrist some prescription drugs to try. As long as Rick takes them, and as long as the doctors get the meds right, Rick is fine. If he's not taking them, or the doctors are trying something new, things can get bad.

Really bad.

Rick puts all his troubles on his job loss and Barack Obama, but I know there is something chemical there. When they work, Rick's medications aren't just pills. They are the vehicle God uses to make Rick whole. That might sound crazy, but it's not. It means that God uses science to fix us and heal us.

Science, and belief. Belief that your family will make it, that struggles happen for a reason, belief that this is the best possible life you can live, so you better find the joy in it. Belief in your marriage, and belief that your husband is a good man and is telling you the truth. I've never had a reason to doubt Rick. I'll take him at his word that he hates Mexicans and isn't a pervert about Marina.

(How do you make the sound of gross? Eecchhh? Egggcchhh? Whatever that sound is, that's what that sentence makes me feel. Hey, Theresa from high school? Guess what? My husband is a member of the Klan, but he's faithful. Jealous? Yeah, you're jealous.)

But I'm going to believe. I'm going to believe my husband is obsessed with my neighbor because of her skin color and his bigotry and not the way she looks in a bathing suit, and, *and*, I'm going to believe that God is going to touch his heart and make him a better man. I'm going to believe God will send the right boat, or the right helicopter.

Belief.

Some love, but a little belief.

And a lot of science.

Chapter Seventeen

Kevin

Two years ago, Marina made something clear to me: anger-management counseling was non-negotiable. Angry at my boss, I had thrown a coffee mug through our kitchen window. It was either go see a shrink or face the possibility of eventually losing my wife and three kids. I love Marina more than anything and wasn't going to be the type of dad who saw his kids every other Wednesday. So, I went to see Dr. Nick, who spoke softly and had a beard that somehow made him look less threatening and less masculine—which I thought defeated the whole point of having a beard.

Dr. Nick opened the session with a simple question.

"Kevin, where do you think your anger comes from?"

I don't know, Doc.

But let me take a crack at it.

Maybe it's the fact that before I was ever born my grandfather molested, impregnated, and ruined my mom.

Maybe it's the fact that my brother and I have gotten more than one birthday present from the landfill. Literally, we shopped at the dump for birthday toys.

Maybe it's the fact that I realized long ago that growing up poor and on welfare is like a terrible secret everyone can see written all over your face.

Buy the wrong shirt? The wrong shoes? The wrong car? Ha! Ha! Ha!

"We knew it all along," they'll say. "Nothing's changed. You're still the kid who used to get dropped off at school in the disgusting green truck wearing a coat you bought at Kmart on layaway and carrying a government cheese sandwich."

Maybe it's the fact that you thought if you married a pretty girl completely unlike your ruined mother, became the first person in your family to go to college and grad school, learned which fork is the salad fork, trained yourself to use chopsticks and order expensive sushi, own t-shirts with the sleeves still attached, spend hundreds of dollars on a haircut, buy expensive shoes, force yourself to drink wine when all you really want is a Coors, read only books with little decals that show they've won an award, never admit to liking *Roseanne*, pretend to like independent films with ambiguous endings, use words like ambiguous, get a manicure, act like you're not disappointed when the waiter brings you a hundred dollar meal on a mostly empty plate, never reference a Jeff Foxworthy joke, get yourself a skin-care routine, refrain from using words like "pertneer" and "ain't" the way your parents did—if you do all those things and a thousand more, maybe people won't know you're just poor welfare trash.

Except they will.

Oh, Dr. Nick, they will.

It's a stink that gets on you and never leaves. You can eat all the sushi you want. You can earn a stack of college degrees so high you can sit on it. You can drive a fleet of expensive German cars. You can wear whatever, buy whatever, earn whatever—and still, people will smell it on you. You didn't inherit money. You didn't inherit a family name. You inherited liking Coors and Jeff Foxworthy and Hank Williams, Jr. You inherited *Roseanne* and sleeveless t-shirts. You inherited the stink you get from growing up broke and on the dole.

The dole. That's what my grandfather called it, like this monster had nothing to do with my mom being on the dole in the first place.

"Margaret, I raised you better than to live off the dole," the Monster used to say to my mom.

When people smell the dole on you, they'll tell you that you don't belong, you're not wanted. And being told you don't belong, that your kind isn't wanted—again—will fill you with rage.

One more thing, Dr. Nick. Can I tell you a little story? It might give you some insight into this anger thing of mine we've been talking about. When I was a freshman in high school, fifteen years old, right after I went to the county dentist to get a cavity worked on, my mom punched me in the mouth. Just to see if it would hurt. It did, doc. My bottom lip split wide open. So, I punched her back. We did this while she was driving. I was fifteen when my mom punched me in the face. She was the same age when her father got her pregnant. Not comparing them, but it's kind of like a joke.

Just not a funny one.

But I didn't tell Dr. Nick any of that. I didn't tell Dr. Nick what it was like growing up on welfare and the way the world makes you feel about your family needing a little help. I didn't tell him about my mom punching me in the mouth, just to see if it would hurt. I kept all that inside. Where it belongs.

Where I can manage it. Where I can control it.

I told Dr. Nick what he wanted to hear: I would meditate. I would breathe. I would go home and tell Marina I was working on it, that it was all under control. I was under control. There was no need to fear me. I am not a dangerous man. I would never throw a coffee cup through our kitchen window again. I promised her that, and I've kept that promise.

Even though I've kept my promise, I haven't let the anger go. I don't want to let it go. Anger can be a valuable emotion in a world that chews people like my family up and spits them out. A little more rage might have kept my parents from ending up constantly on the short end of life.

I learned a valuable lesson the afternoon I used my fist to bounce my mom's head off the window of her Grand Am.

You don't let someone cross a line. And you always, always hit back.

Rick

I know how to make a yard sign.

First, you pray for the right message. When the message arrives, you take your Dodge Neon down to Home Depot and buy some supplies. Nails. A piece of plywood. Spray-paint. A hammer. You already have a hammer, but your arrogant neighbor bought a new hammer when he put up his sign, so you buy a new hammer too.

You take your supplies home, storing them on the top shelf in your garage so your wife doesn't find them. While she sleeps, you get to work. First, the spray-paint. Then the nails. Then the hammer. Quietly though, so you don't wake your daughters. Or your wife. You walk out to your front yard, making sure your maniac of a neighbor isn't watching you.

By the time you're done it's nearly light out, so you get to see the look on your neighbor's face when he sees what you've done as he climbs into his brand-new truck. It's a look that makes you know all your hard work was worth it. He looks sick with rage when he reads it.

If you don't want to get
LOCKED
in a cage
STAY IN YOUR OWN COUNTRY!!!!!!!!
#MAGA
#LOCKTHEMUP
#LOCKHERUP

Marina

Text Message Sent at 8:44 PM
Rick! It's Marina. Can we talk?

8:52 PM
Rick it's Marina. I tried you on Facebook. Please text me.

8:59 PM
Hey Rick! I really need to talk to you

9:21 PM
please we need to stop this before someone gets hurt

9:47 PM
I'll be at Beans, the coffee shop tomorrow morning if you want to talk

Kate

I know how to break a heart.

First, you start with a girl who meets the love of her life when she's just ten years old. Before high school the girl decides this boy will one day be the man she builds a life with. They get pregnant before they're even married, which they've been taught is a sin. It's hard for the girl to wrap her mind around the idea that an act of love with a man she loves is a sin, but she has accepted Jesus Christ as her Lord and Savior. The girl understands that He knows better than her about what makes a life a Godly life.

She and the young man she loves are forgiven. They get married. But the man is still a man and sometimes he stumbles. When he stumbles, she stands by her husband and the father of her girls.

"Poco a poco," he'll say.

Little by little. She accepts that life with this man will always be a struggle of little by little.

That's okay though, because she loves her man. She stands by her man. She's proud of that.

She stands by her man when he's diagnosed with a mental illness and can't have the patriotic war hero life he always wanted. She stands by her man when he chooses a career that leaves their growing family forever struggling, always balancing mortgage payments against medical bills against car payments on a used Dodge Neon. She stands by her man when he loses his job for what he calls a joke, a joke she worries was not funny at all. She stands by her man when she finds a rifle in the garage and worries that he had the barrel of that rifle in his mouth the night before. She stands by her man when he embarrasses his wife and daughters with profane tirades and crazy behavior on Facebook.

She stands by her man because they've loved each other since they were just children. She stands by her man because theirs is a Godly love. She stands by her man because she believes God will eventually show her husband how special and wonderful this life—this hard life they've been blessed to live together—really is. She stands by her man because she believes with God's guidance, her husband will stop focusing so much on politics. She stands by her man because she believes he will eventually stop watching so much news and spending so much time on the Internet and focus instead on his wife and daughters, like he used to.

She stands by her man because, despite his many faults, he is loyal. Her man is hers and only hers. People like her and her husband have to earn a good life—even a hard, good life—and she will not allow anyone to take her husband or this life from her. She believes her man when he tells her his heart and his body belong only to her. She believes him when he says he looks at the neighbor woman because she's a Mexican and he hates Mexicans, and not because the neighbor woman is so much prettier and younger than she is and doesn't look like she's had one baby, let alone a whole house full.

The neighbor woman has had an easy life with lots of money and little hardship, and it shows on her wrinkle-free face and perfect body.

She believes her husband when he looks her in the eye and says, "Katie, you know what me and my brothers call women like Marina? Boner killer. Total boner killer." She believes him because when they giggle about this dirty word spoken in the daylight, life feels as good as it almost always has between the two of them. When they laugh together, she can see the boy she fell in love with and the man she's growing old with. She stands by her man because she believes the husband she loves is still somewhere inside the profane person she saw holding a rifle while cursing out a computer screen. How do you destroy that strong of belief? How do you weaken a love everyone believes is indestructible? How do you make a woman wonder if all this trouble is worth it, if she wouldn't be better off taking her bigger paycheck and their girls and seeing if they can make it on their own?

How do you break a heart?

I know how.

You lie to your wife, and, maybe, maybe you lie to yourself. Maybe you put the new sign up to send a message to the neighbor you're having a feud with. Maybe you put the sign up to distract your wife from whatever you have going on with the neighbor woman, the one you've been watching sunbathe and prance around in a bikini since the day she moved here.

The woman who couldn't take her eyes off of you at the dinner party. The woman who has a BMW and fake breasts and a clean house and cucumber melon water on her counter and a husband who is perfect. Completely perfect. The woman who has all of that and still isn't satisfied, so she tries to take what isn't hers. The woman who's trying to grab something she has no right to grab.

Maybe, Rick, maybe you put your crazy sign up because you actually do hate Mexicans *and* to throw me off the trail and make me believe you don't have something going on with Marina. Maybe it's both.

Life, after all, can be binary.

You can't lie to me anymore, Rick. I don't believe you. I was a stand-by-my-man woman.

Right up until the moment I checked your phone and found out that the thing you couldn't make work for me—the soft thing you held in your hand as you cried and told me it wasn't me, that I was still beautiful to you—seemed to be working just fine for Marina.

Chapter Eighteen

Kate

I was on Marina's side of the street with a butcher knife in my hand before I even thought twice about what I had seen on my husband's phone.

Beans?

Beans?

Where a simple cup of coffee costs six dollars? Where they serve chicken Applewood sausage fancy-schmancy breakfast sandwiches for nine dollars? The place we only took our daughters for graduations and birthdays? Marina ate at Beans on a normal weekday? With my Rick? She was going to show my Rick what his life could be like while looking into her perfect store-bought cleavage and eating chicken Applewood sausage?

HECK NO.

She wasn't taking this from me. She wasn't taking him from me. I didn't know what I planned on doing when I got inside her house, but I knew one thing—Marina was never going to text my husband again. This was stopping tonight.

That's when I noticed Marina must have left their side yard gate open. I went through it, and a few feet from their sliding glass door I realized her twelve-hundred-dollar dog was outside, looking up at me.

Who leaves the gate open with a twelve-hundred-dollar dog in the backyard? Especially when the dog is barely bigger than a kitten? I'll tell you who. Someone who is so sure her dog will never find greener grass in another yard that she doesn't even need to close the gate. Someone who doesn't understand or appreciate how much twelve-hundred-dollars really is.

The dog looked up at me, her jeweled collar sparkling in the moonlight, her sweater keeping her warm on a night when no sweater was even needed. The dog let out a single, sharp-sounding bark. She was telling the neighborhood I was a threat. She was warning me to stay away.

"Quiet JK. You know me," I whispered.

She barked again as I peered through Marina's kitchen window, looking for any sign that she might be awake. This would be a lot easier if I didn't have to go looking for her.

"JK! Bad girl. Be quiet. You know me!"

She barked again.

"Stop it! I am your neighbor! From across the street! You know me!"

She barked again.

That's when I picked JK up by her sparkly collar and drove the butcher knife through her throat. The knife went all the way through, coming out the other side. There was a single whimper, much quieter than her warning bark. A knife through the throat is a lot quieter way to die than you would think, if you were the type of person to think about those things. JK went limp in my hand. She died a quick death in her own yard at the hand of her neighbor from across the street.

I'm not sure how long I stood there. While I know it couldn't have been long, it was long enough for a little bit of the fog to lift. There I was, in my neighbor's yard, in my pajamas, with a bloody butcher knife in my hand and a dead dog at my feet. A really expensive dead dog. Even if I didn't go to jail for this, there was no way we could afford to replace her dog. Plus, I would be a monster. I would be the crazy lady who killed a kitten-sized dog with a butcher knife. In the middle of the night.

Even from the Harrisons' side yard I could see the homemade sign my husband made telling our neighborhood we think people should be locked up in cages. If anyone knew I did this, we would no longer be the Sullivans, hosts of a wonderful Fall Harvest party. We would be the monsters down the street.

This isn't who we are. At least this isn't who I ever thought Rick and I would be. People like us— me and Rick, Marina and Kevin—we didn't kill dogs and threaten each other on Facebook. We are nice families in the suburbs. We aren't animals from the city. There are people like us and people like that. We aren't people like that. At least I thought we weren't.

I had to get out of their side yard and get the blood off me, but I didn't know if the girls would be awake from the barking or not. I couldn't walk back into the house with a bloody butcher knife in my hand. Truthfully, I could probably kill a person and be forgiven by the girls quicker than I would be for killing a dog, especially that dog. When Marina first got JK, the girls loved to go over to the Harrisons' house to play with her puppy and drink lemonade.

I didn't run back home. I laid JK down, careful not to just drop her, and walked away quickly. Running would look suspicious. I kept the knife in my hand as I crossed the street, not realizing until much too late that the blade dripped a trail of JK's blood from the Harrisons' yard to our garage door. Thankfully JK hadn't woken Rick or the girls. Our garage was open. It was the first time I was ever grateful that Rick could be so forgetful about closing it. I put the bloody butcher knife in the Neon's glovebox. I didn't have a change of clothes. I had no idea where I was going. Luckily there was a twenty-dollar bill in the cupholder.

Thank God for small miracles.

I didn't turn the car's headlights on until I was outside of our neighborhood. I kept driving until I got to a truck stop thirty miles away. In the parking lot I cried harder than I have ever cried before. My tears smeared with the blood on my hands and face until I looked like something out of a horror movie.

I prayed to God for some way to make this right. I prayed for the Neon to be a time machine so I could travel back to a Fall Harvest party a few years ago, the first one Kevin and Marina attended. I would spend the whole time getting to know them better. I would ask Marina where she was from, if she grew up in Mexico. I would ask her for a good taco recipe. If we understood each other, maybe Kevin and Rick wouldn't get in crazy Facebook fights. Maybe they wouldn't have stupid sign wars. Maybe Marina would know how important this life is to me. Maybe she never would have tried to get Rick to meet her for a coffee date.

A lifetime of maybes.

But a Dodge Neon isn't a time machine. It's just a piece of junk little car. A piece of junk we still make payments on. In another world what happened that night and what came after could all be avoided. In this world though, no matter how hard I prayed, it was just too late.

Marina

Normally, I wake up in the morning and let JK outside to pee. While my coffee brews I stand in the side yard, watching the sunrise and trying to justify to myself why a cigarette before the kids wake up is a perfectly okay thing to do. Once I let JK back inside she runs into Becky's room and climbs under the blankets, curling up behind our oldest daughter's knee. If JK can't find Becky she'll look for Eliza or Kevin Jr.

That morning I walked upstairs and called her name.

"JK! Let's go outside! Mommy's awake."

Nothing.

"JK! Come on baby! Mommy's awake!"

Nothing.

"JK! Kevin! Becky! Have you seen JK?"

Nothing.

"Kevin! Have you seen JK?"

I had this nightmarish image of my husband letting our dog out to pee, forgetting to shut the gate, and then falling asleep.

I checked the front yard.

Nothing.

I checked the backyard.

Nothing.

I opened the door to the side yard, and that's when I saw her. Kevin had remembered to let JK out to pee—he just hadn't remembered to let her back in.

My puppy was very bloody, and obviously very dead.

What happened next was all a blur. I screamed. I didn't scream words, just an incoherent yell. Maybe I screamed for Kevin, I don't remember. I forgot what time it was. I didn't know if the kids were awake or asleep, at school or in their bedrooms. I ran over to JK, not caring if her blood got all over me.

Something was wrong with her throat, and when I picked her up her head felt loose on her neck. I staggered around to the front yard, where I fell to my knees. My tears mixed with JK's blood to make my face a disgusting, scary mess.

I didn't know what to do. I didn't want the kids to see me like this.

I screamed Kevin's name, and that's when our front door opened. My husband ran right by me, letting out his own scream, something large and silver in his hand, his eyes fixed on a trail of blood that went from our house to the Sullivans. I guess in my heart I knew what was in Kevin's hand, but everything was moving too quickly. By the time I screamed, my husband was already in the street, and Rick was coming out of his garage, heading straight toward Kevin with a rifle in his hands. It looked like Rick had been crying, but that might have just been the tears in my own eyes blurring my vision. I pulled JK closer to me, knowing she was dead, but still needing her, still needing anyone.

Then I heard a sound that made me think of being a child, and my mother telling me rain was God's tears. The sound that came from our street that morning was like God's fist slamming down on a table, telling us She had had quite enough.

Though I loved her so much, hearing God's fist made JK not seem quite as important.

That didn't stop me from holding her in my arms as I ran toward the body of my husband, and the body of a man I barely knew.

Part III: The Aftermath

Chapter Nineteen

Marina

We.

A single two-letter word was my biggest mistake. It wasn't my only mistake, but it was by far the biggest. If I hadn't used the word "We" in my text messages, things might be so different. If I would have said "Rick, the four of us need to talk this out" instead of "Rick! It's Marina. Can we talk?" Kate wouldn't have thought Rick and I were having an affair.

And Kevin might still be alive.

Why did I use that word "we?" Because to me, the four of us were a We. Not a We like me and Kevin were a We. The four of us had our problems, but we were still something more than strangers. We lived on the same street. Our children attended the same schools. We literally breathed the same air. I thought people like us could work things out without guns and knives and dead dogs and dead husbands. I was wrong.

It was too late for us to be a We.

Why did I text Rick, and not Kate? Why didn't I try talking to my own husband, rather than the man across the street? I didn't try talking to Kate because I knew exactly what she thought of me before everything fell apart. I wasn't Marina the Mexican to her. I wasn't even Marina, the slightly-tanner-than-normal white girl. I was Marina, the spoiled trophy wife who had nothing better to do than sit on the front porch and sunbathe while her husband spied on me through the window.

Why didn't I talk to Kevin? I did. I tried. When it came to Rick, my husband was well beyond reason. He was ready for that morning. When he saw me with JK's bloody little body in my arms, that was the end. I have no idea where the gun came from, but the look on his face made me understand Kevin had been waiting for this moment his entire life. He was looking for a reason to settle a score, to right wrongs that had made him so angry for so long. Some of the wrongs were about Rick, but most of them went back a long time. Long before Rick. Long before me.

Long before Kevin himself.

I screamed a second time when I saw Rick come out of his garage with a rifle in his hands. Kevin didn't register my scream. It all happened so fast.

When I looked up Kevin was already on the ground. My husband died instantly, but not before firing his own shot. Kevin's anger couldn't or wouldn't let him hear me.

That sort of sums up my husband's life.

I know now he could never escape his childhood, or at least his perception of his childhood. His parents struggled with addiction, they were often poor, and his mom was broken beyond repair. All true. All horrific. What he could never see was that he had long ago transcended his childhood. He was no longer the poor welfare kid. He stopped being that person right around the time he graduated from college. He stopped being that person right around the time he met me and Becky.

He had a life other people could only imagine.

What I wish, with all my heart, is that Kevin could have seen himself the way I saw him. Before his anger overtook him, he was my hero. I know that's not an empowered thing to say, but it's true. He was my hero, and he wasn't my hero because he rescued me from being a single-mom, or because he became Becky's dad. I loved him for those things, but I never needed to be rescued. I could make my own way in the world. I did it before I met him, and I'll have to do it now. I have no other choice.

Kevin was my hero because when he decided something was going to happen, it was going to happen. He decided he was going to graduate from college, and it happened. He decided he was going to have a successful career, and that happened. He decided he would build a family that was secure and safe and never had to worry about where their food was coming from or whether the power would get shut off, and that happened. He decided he was going to earn a life where he could buy his kids and his wife anything they needed—except his time—and that happened.

But the first thing he decided he was going to have was me.

When we met, I was still recovering from my divorce from the shithead, and I told him that. He didn't care. He showed up while I was on shift with a little stuffed bear for Becky. He called. He asked me out for coffee. He even bought me tampons when I couldn't get out of the house because Becky had an ear infection. Kevin was relentless in everything, even his love.

Three months later we were married, and I knew that the life and family we would create together would be all I ever wanted. Back then I still believed Kevin would one day feel the same way, that one day his beautiful wife and beautiful children would be enough.

I used to daydream about the perfect day I wished for my husband. He would have a great workout and stop on the way back to his apartment at a little diner with outdoor seating. He would be looking off in the distance, waiting for his protein shake and egg white omelet, when something would catch his eye on the horizon. While looking at that spot in the sky, all his rage would be lifted away. There would be no more bitter jokes about government cheese, no obsession with creating a family name, no mugs thrown through kitchen windows, no pretending to like wine and sad movies while pretending to hate stupid sitcoms and cheap steaks and anything else his parents loved. There would be no wars with neighbors, no hate-filled Facebook exchanges. All of that would be gone. Later that night he would meet a girl who had a little girl of her own, and they would fall in love. He would finish college and decide he wanted a boring job. Maybe he would be an accountant. Maybe he would be a salesman. He would work just enough to pay for a mortgage on a little house where he and the girl would raise their family. He wouldn't care how much his car or haircut cost. His hair and his cars would say nothing about him, at least nothing worth knowing.

The only thing that would say anything about this Kevin was how much his wife and children adored him. And it wouldn't matter who was President. Well, it would, in the way that things are supposed to matter when you're an adult. But like expensive jeans, whoever was President wouldn't say anything about Kevin or his childhood. Whoever it was would just be the President, and in four years or eight years he or she would be gone.

Eventually those four years would stack up and up, and one day he wouldn't look forward to the next election because it was time slipping away, and he would be old enough to understand how valuable time is. He would know the time together with these people who loved him was precious, and one day it would be gone forever. But that would be okay, because seeing a long, hard, beautiful life wind down isn't the worst thing. At least he had the chance to grow old with a woman who thought a man with a boring job was her hero.

It would be the day he met me.

It would be a long day, filled with dates at the dollar theater and picnics and used cars and learning how to fix our house as it broke down and graduations and grandkids and saving up for cheap vacations and a love that mattered more than what anyone thought of us. Our love would matter more than our last name going on a street sign. Our love would be our legacy.

It would be our perfect day.

And it would last for a very long time.

Kate

By God's grace. Lord willing.

Me and Rick would say those things to help us understand our own lives. We said those things because it helped us make peace with hardship. Lord willing, one day we would drive a car that didn't shake uncontrollably when it went over fifty miles an hour. By God's grace, we had a car at all.

Always wanting more. Always settling for less. Grace.

I don't think I ever really understood the meaning of that word until Marina forgave me for killing JK. When I got back from the truck stop, Marina crossed the street to give me a hug. It was the first time we'd ever hugged. It was the first time we ever touched each other at all. Even when Kevin's mom died, all I did was hand her a casserole and wish her a safe trip. What I wouldn't give to go back in time and change that. Marina didn't forgive me for JK right away, but when Rick's life insurance paid out, I bought Marina a new puppy. Twelve hundred dollars for a dog. That's crazy.

But she was worth every penny.

I knew by the time I got back to the house how stupid it was to think my Rick would throw away everything we worked for on an affair with the neighbor. His role in what happened wasn't about attraction to Marina. It was about his obsession with politics and his illness.

And his racism.

I'm no dummy. I knew who and what my husband was, but because he was mine I was willing to look the other way on his obsessions, his illness, his bigotry, and all his other flaws. I had something in this world no one could take away. Then I read his text messages, and thought Marina was trying to take him from me. Marina, who I knew I could never compete with. Marina, who had a life I only wished I could have.

Our family made it work for years by never buying new cars and only going to the discount movie theater and, except for our honeymoon, never taking a fancy-schmancy vacation. For a moment I had a butcher knife in my hand and was so angry that I survived all the years of struggle, just to see Marina come to a place that wasn't hers and take what she had no right to take.

I've never been that angry before. I hated the way it felt.

By the time I got back to the house to find my husband and a neighbor I hardly knew dead on our street, I realized how stupid that was, how stupid and petty I had been. Marina was just trying to live her life. Then I killed her dog, and because I killed her dog, the next morning I arrived at a crime scene and the end of my life as I knew it.

The girls and I will survive. That's what women do. But we will never get back what we lost.

I have a pretty good idea why Rick was in the garage with his rifle. I don't think it had anything to do with Kevin, Marina, JK, or a murder. He woke up and I was gone. Maybe he thought I was having breakfast with a friend. Maybe he thought I was at a parent-teacher conference. But maybe he thought I had had enough of his war with Kevin and the humiliating signs and Facebook fights. Maybe he thought I had left him. Maybe it wasn't any of those things. Maybe the voices in his head said something so crazy and illogical that he decided it was just time to quiet them. I didn't have my phone with me that night, so I'll never know what he would have said if he had reached me any of the eight times he called.

I think my husband planned on shooting someone. It just wasn't Kevin. I think he had the rifle in his mouth when he heard Kevin yelling and Marina screaming, and everything spun out of control. A fight between two neighbors had gotten to the point where neither side could restrain themselves, and action and reactions fed off each other. The result was two dead husbands in body bags. The police don't know who shot who first, and I don't really care.

The result is the same. The love of my life is gone. The life I loved is gone.

I know what people think about my husband. Rick was a fanatic and a bigot if you watch some channels, a hero and a freedom fighter if you watch others. My Rick wasn't a fanatic, a hero, or a freedom fighter. He was a bigot, but if you live long enough you'll learn that the same man who thinks it's okay to say awful things about blacks and Mexicans can be the same man who buys a homeless guy a hot dog. That was my Rick. Even if the homeless guy was black or Chinese, Rick would buy him a hot dog and a Pepsi.

It's like some of the boys in my class who come from rough homes in the ghetto. They'll start the school year by walking up and punching someone, just as a warning to other boys about not crossing a line. But I'll see those same boys tying their little brother's shoelace or holding their sister's hand as they cross the street together.

People aren't just one thing.

Rick wasn't just the worst parts of himself. In the end he might have become a monster I didn't know. That doesn't mean he became a monster I didn't love. He's a stereotype now. A story. A meme. For the rest of their lives, my girls will google their own names and find articles about their father, the bigot/hero/lunatic. They will live in the shadow of a father who never wanted to cast a shadow, who just wanted to raise his girls and be a reporter in his little hometown.

I wish it was different. I wish they could google him and read about the night we went to Olive Garden to celebrate his first year at the paper. The Garden was big spending for us. That night we were at our table, making the all-you-can-eat breadsticks last, when someone passed by and recognized Rick.

"Mr. Sullivan, I loved your piece on the parade," the man said. "So much history there. The story really needs to get told, right? Anyway, have a great dinner."

When we went to pay we found out the man who liked the parade story had already bought our dinner. Rick was glowing. He was important enough for someone to buy a meal for him and his wife. He never wanted to be more than that: important enough for a pat on the back, an atta boy, a free meal at the Olive Garden in the town he loved.

He didn't want to be more than that, but I don't think he could be less than that, either.

It's easy to judge my husband. It's easy to wonder how someone could be so angry over losing so little. An Assistant Editor job at a little local paper? That's worth losing your bearings over? That's worth showing the world your worst side? Couldn't you see Facebook was going to put you out of a job? Couldn't you read the writing on the wall?

But maybe the people who say that just haven't lost anything that really mattered to them. When the paper closed, Rick didn't just lose something that mattered to him. In his mind, Rick lost mattering at all. Then he lost the job that followed and ended up selling toilet paper, and at every step along the way his paycheck became smaller and smaller.

It makes me so sad that the myth Rick has become after he died matters so much more than the man he was. The real Rick will always be a part of my story. Who was the real Rick? The real Rick took me out west for our honeymoon. It was a long drive in a beat-up Ford Ranger.

We barely had any money, and the first night we slept in the back of the truck. I was pregnant. It was horrible. I didn't get any sleep at all and had to constantly lower myself in and out of the Ranger to take a tinkle by the tire. I told Rick I wasn't going to sleep in that truck bed again. Rick could see I was miserable. The next night we checked into a Holiday Inn. The real Rick loved me and wanted me to be happy. That night I was really, really happy. It was the most expensive hotel we ever stayed in. I curled up in nice sheets, the air conditioning running full blast, my new husband's arm around my pregnant belly and his mustache tickling my ear as he whispered how much he loved me and told me about the wonderful life we would have together.

It was a perfect night.

Lord willing, after I leave this world years from now I will feel Rick's belly pressed against my back, his mustache against my ear as he whispers how much he loves me.

By God's grace, I will keep the memory of our night in the Holiday Inn with me every day, until I see my husband again.

Kevin and Rick

www.mitchellfuneralhomes.com

Kevin Michael Harrison tragically left this world on Tuesday, November 11. Kevin was born to Robert and Margaret Harrison on March 13, 1981. He graduated from Central High School in Denver before moving to Flagstaff, Arizona, to attend college. It was there he met his wife, Marina, and her daughter, Becky. These women were the two great loves of his life. Everyone who knew him knew how much he loved his instant family. Kevin would later adopt Becky, and he and Marina would have two more children, Kevin Jr. and Eliza.

Kevin was a loving husband, father, son, and brother. He will be remembered for his passion, his desire to make the world a better place, and his love of family. He worked harder than anyone he knew and believed hard work was the only way to overcome adversity. He is survived by his brother, Cory, his cousin, Lance, and his father, Robert. Kevin was preceded in death by his mother, Margaret.

Kevin's family will hold an open house this Saturday, November 21, at 6311 Highland Road. They welcome anyone who would like to attend.

www.mitchellfuneralhomes.com

Richard "Rick" Allen Sullivan met his Lord and Savior on November 11. Rick was born to David and Cybil Sullivan on July 6, 1968. Rick graduated from Robert Kennedy High School before attending and graduating from his beloved "U." Rick met his wife Katherine (Kate) in middle school, and she was the love of his life. Their marriage produced four beautiful daughters, Anna (Mark) Freiderman, Kelly, Madison, and Peyton.

Rick was a devoted and loving father, husband, brother, and uncle. Rick was a man of God who served his community. He was a man of strong convictions who believed in hard work, honor, and commitment. For most of his career, Rick served as Assistant Editor of the *Daily Post*. It was in this job that he was most fulfilled. Rick is survived by his brothers, Robert, Michael, Terry, and Matthew, his sisters, Mary and Sarah, and too many cousins to count.

Rick's family will hold a reception on Thursday, November 19, at 6314 Highland Road and would love it if his community attended and enjoyed one another's company.

Chapter Twenty

Marina & Kate

Once Kevin and Rick shot each other, they realized they knew all they needed to know about us.

Who's they? The talking heads. The tweeters, or whatever you call them. The brave, anonymous souls writing in comment sections, trashing people they've never met.

They knew Kevin was a kid who rose from a humble, difficult upbringing to become a shining example of everything a modern man should be: Tolerant. Open-minded. Non-judgmental. Educated. Healthy. Well-adjusted. Non-violent. A driver of foreign cars. An eater of arugula and a watcher of *Queer Eye.* He had great hair, supported gay marriage, and had black friends. He knew how to order a good steak. He even married an immigrant woman, as if there could be no greater example of a white American male's transcendence into something more than just a run-of-the-mill deplorable than managing to find a brown woman attractive.

(Penises being well known for their rigid respect for boundaries of race, color, and nationality.)

They knew enough to know Kevin was their hero. He was everything they wanted him to be, and so much more.

They knew Kevin was an overeducated elitist born into a life of privilege. Need evidence? Read the interview where his dad talks about how proud he was of Kevin for earning three college degrees. Who needs three college degrees? What you're looking at in that interview is unearned privilege being handed down from one generation of snowflake to the next. To top it all off, he married an immigrant who had a baby with another man. Before she met this privileged monster, his immigrant bride even used the state healthcare program to keep her anchor baby from getting ear infections. Kevin Harrison was a hypocrite, too—look at what he allegedly believed about women's rights, and yet he kept his wife at home, practically barefoot and chained to a stove. At the same time, he hated traditional family values. We don't even need to tell you that. Just look at his mixed, blended family. Its existence undermines everything God wants a family to be.

They knew enough to know Kevin Harrison was the villain they were already looking for. He was exactly what was wrong with this country, and so much more.

They knew Rick was a hard-working, God-fearing, blue-collar, American family man. He was exactly what this country was built on. He didn't drive a fancy car. He ate lettuce, not arugula. He was the last of a dying breed, a hard-working white American male who could be the bread-winner for his family without needing some fancy elitist education. He was the forgotten man. If our country was ever going to get back on track, it was because of men like Rick Sullivan. Racism? That sign wasn't racism. Those Facebook posts had nothing to do with racism or sexism or any other ism. It was all about economic anxiety. Rick Sullivan didn't hate brown people.

(People like Rick Sullivan don't hate brown people, the cable news talking heads said. They just feel threatened by an economy that is leaving them behind. You're asking about the sign? Again? That sign wasn't hate. It was free speech. It's what the troops are out there defending. You do love the troops, don't you?)

They knew enough to know Rick was their hero. He was everything they wanted him to be, and so much more.

They knew Rick was a disgusting example of the worst type of deplorable. It wouldn't matter if Rick were alive. You wouldn't need to get to know him. You already knew all you needed to know. Rick Sullivan hated the environment. Rick Sullivan hated poor people. Rick Sullivan hated healthcare for everyone. Rick Sullivan was never, ever welcoming to his neighbors. Kevin Harrison bent over backwards to try and get to know Rick Sullivan, but Rick could never get past the fact that Kevin married an immigrant. Rick Sullivan hated them from the beginning. He practically burned a cross on the Harrisons' yard the day they moved there. Even worse, Rick Sullivan practically kept his own wife and daughter in burkas. Rick Sullivan didn't have a single friend in the whole town.

They knew enough to know Rick was their villain. He was exactly what was wrong with this country, and so much more.

They knew enough to know Marina was the noble immigrant woman who practically arrived here in middle America soaking wet with a baby on her back, helpless until she was rescued by this modern American man, this white Obama. They knew enough to know she came here looking to undermine and destroy everything they loved about this country. She was a Latina Jihadist, born to destroy the Fourth of July.

They knew enough to know Kate was the consummate homemaker, an example of a woman who could balance God and a career and biblical loyalty to her husband. Jealousy? Envy? No. No way. Her life was everything she had ever prayed for. The refugee woman across the street was no competition for Kate Sullivan, and she knew it. They knew enough to know Kate was an example of everything that holds women back. Subservient to her husband, she was what he told her to be. She was too busy baking him a cake to ever get woke. It was all politics. No mental illness. No bathroom sink covered with prescription medication bottles. No mother who had to figure out how to raise sons in a violent world after she experienced so much sexual violence at the hands of her father, a man who was also once someone's son. No rapidly changing economy leaving middle-aged workers behind. No loss of a job and a career you used to love. No smartphones pumping endless amounts of bad news into our pockets twenty-four hours a day. No cable channels making billions of dollars by telling us who to fear and who to hate.

Just left versus right.

Once they realized they knew all they needed to know, the four of us weren't human beings.

We were an excuse. An excuse to scream louder, to inch even closer to the brink.

Us?

We're going to stick together. In the year since our husbands died, we've taken the pieces of two broken families and made something new. Not something better, really. As flawed as they were, we miss our husbands. Every day. But we've made something different. We are a new kind of we, and even if we will always mourn what we lost, new and different can be good.

We're headed out west. We're headed out west because one of us has never seen the ocean, and we hope it's as blue and as pretty as she always imagined it. We're headed out west because it's never a bad idea to be near the water if things in this country get even crazier. If that happens the ocean could be an escape—but if two old mothers (well, oldish mothers), six strong young women, a son-in-law, a teenage boy, a baby, and one tiny dog are climbing into a raft and taking their chances on the Pacific, things have gotten even worse than they are now.

Who knows?

Maybe the apocalypse has already started. Maybe the end began when so many of us started believing that the only thing that defines a person is who they vote for. If that's the case, we'll figure things out. We will make our way. Maybe we will cross the Pacific on a raft and open a hardware store when we get to the other side.

El pequeño jefe señoras.

Las dos pequeñas señoras jefes que vinieron de América.

Poco a poco, we will make it work. People like us are survivors.

But escape isn't really why we want to be by the ocean.

We want to stand on the beach, look toward the horizon and imagine a place where people don't already know all they need to know about their neighbor.

A place where people can still surprise each other.

A place that isn't this close to the brink.

~ End ~

12374361R00134